SNAP
SLICE

JIM SUTHERLAND

SNAP SLICE

Copyright © 2013 by Jim Sutherland

First Print Edition

Originally published as STACK AND TILT, THE NOVEL

Cover design by Doris Cheung. www.dorischeungartmedia.com
Biography photo by Paul Joseph. www.pjoseph.com
Layout by 52 Novels. www.52novels.com

ISBN 978-0-9919366-2-5

CollingwoodBooks

Vancouver
www.collingwoodbooks.com.

To Jessie, John and Ira, with love.
And to my mom, who as a librarian knows that the pages of a book
are exactly the place for behavior of this sort.

ACKNOWLEDGEMENTS

Jokes, anecdotes and situations have been borrowed from the words and actions of golf partners that include Jack MacDermot and Ed Giovenella, among others. Fellow dinner party guests and poker players, likewise. Grateful thanks to all. A special shout-out to Laurel Wellman for making a whole lot of things better and cleaner. Additional thanks to Chris Dafoe for his legal advice and Amy Siders for her publishing expertise. Doris Cheung's cover is simply brilliant. And Google and Wikipedia, you're the best.

1-4/3
Flagstick Stuck into Green Some Distance from Hole by Practical Joker

Q. A practical joker removes the flagstick from the hole and sticks it into the putting green some distance from the hole. The players playing toward the green are unaware of this action and they play toward the flagstick and not the hole. Do the players have the option to replay?

A. No. In equity (Rule 1-4) the players must accept the resultant advantage or disadvantage."

—Decisions on the Rules of Golf

CHAPTER 1
THAT'S NOT WHY I CALLED

JEFF, MAY 6, 2007

L et there be no illusions about where I would have landed a year ago on the fucket lists of Dunbar Gates Scratch Club regulars. Somewhere between restoring a Mercury Lynx and learning to cook with moss. Getting up early on a Sunday morning to watch Jeff Jones tee off — just one of the many things to probably not do before you die.

But a few events have transpired in the meantime, as the guys streaming in know. On May 18, 2006, after shooting an all too typical 79 and downing an all too typical three glasses of all too typical Mirror Pond Ale, I untypically poured gasoline through the sunroof of a gunmetal gray SUV and set it ablaze. The cuckold-making circumstances leading up to this act are equally well known, as indeed are the other actors. Syd London, a Dunbar member since the age of eight, is the beloved daughter of Sam London, one of the club's longest standing and most esteemed members. Kevin Howell had just reached the top of the waiting list and been accepted for membership. Any shortfall in the titillation quotient was rectified when the directors elected to circulate the text of proceedings leading to the granting of a court order barring me from the club. They did this, ostensibly, on the grounds that the membership was affected. As a result everyone also knew of a subsequent break-in—perpetrated by person or persons unknown—in which some of Kevin's personal effects had urine poured or otherwise distributed upon them. There was something of a groundswell to have my membership revoked, but because no criminal charges were laid, this lost impetus before coming to a vote.

I was aware of all this due to an email correspondence insisted upon by a fellow member, Art Tallis, who for equally puzzling reasons apparently wishes to remain my friend. And indeed, when I pull up on Sunday morning, Art is standing there by the driveway. He seems more nervous than I am, but he tells me not to worry about a thing. He will be in my foursome, along with Dave "Dude" Smart and someone named Cam Wallace, a guest from a reciprocal club who happens to pull up as I do and quickly falls in with us.

Art stares me up and down, and says I look just great, which seems not in keeping with the usual mano-a-mano Scratch Club style. He helps me pull my bag out of the trunk and we give it to a burly new assistant who, unusually for lackadaisical Dunbar, materializes at just the right moment. On our way in to grab a coffee before heading over for a quick warm-up on the range, I duck into the pro shop and say hello to Ben, who seems flustered and actually apologizes for a joke he made when I called to say I'd be returning to the club. There's a moment to marvel all over again at the mastery of the architect hired to do the clubhouse and pro shop back in 1934. A lesser designer might have driven down the blind alley of art deco, but instead the long forgotten genius somehow reconciled Frank Lloyd Wright with barely emerging modernism, and did this while still celebrating the local Craftsman tradition. So much old-growth, edge-grain fir. So many exquisite details.

The three of us are the first on the range, but within minutes virtually the entire Sunday morning group arrives. To a man they say hello, some stopping to watch as I stripe my 5-iron to within inches of the 200-yard marker six times in succession. This is going well. Oddly well. "Did Ben mention I had a surprise for everyone?" I ask the others in my foursome as we gather at the first tee.

"He did," says Art. "We weren't sure what you meant. What did you mean? To tell you the truth, some people were a little worried."

"Worried? Well, they should be."

"Why do you say that?" interjects Cam, who seems not to understand the fundamental conceit of golf: that by simple virtue of showing up at the course we are transformed into 12-year-olds without a care in the world.

"You saw that 5-iron."

"You have a new 5-iron?"

"No, same old club. I'm just hitting it differently. All my clubs."

"The boys will be relieved," says Art.

"No, they won't."

A half-dozen guys have gathered around to watch by the tee box, which sparks the recognition that I have always resisted an occasional inclination toward the mildest form of cockiness by remembering that I have absolutely nothing to be cocky about. But a new swing isn't the only residual effect of my time in the wilderness. I also spent hour after interminable hour studying the psychology of golf, and armed myself with a new approach to the game, not to mention a new routine.

The function of a routine is to let the muscles take over from the mind, to clear the golfer's head of doubts and distractions, allowing him to focus on the immediate crucial task in a relaxed yet focused way. On Sunday afternoons a TV commentator is more likely to share his growing incontinence concerns than to fail to note the efficacy of a contender's routine.

I developed mine during the course of those hundreds of thousands of swings at the range I have been frequenting for, oh, seven hours a day. One consequence of taking so many reps is that I can remain virtually devoid of swing thoughts; wielding the club is as natural as breathing. The other is a visualization technique I can confidently call unique. Where others imagine the flight of the ball or the patch of ground where it is supposed to land, I will it through the shattered window of an Oldsmobile.

The first hole at Dunbar is a 520-yard par 5, with water pinching in from the right at 240 yards. Dave is first off with a 3-wood that fades a touch but isn't going to hurt him. Although a four or five handicap like me, Art's not long, so he hits his driver, propelling the ball straight down the middle as usual. Cam hops the ball maybe 125 yards into the right rough, which is hardly surprising given a swing that looks like it belongs on an executive course, at best.

What, has Dunbar gone to hell in my absence? Isn't this supposed to be the Scratch Club, the cherished reserve of single-digit handicaps? I know little of Cam's own club on the other side of town, but I can imagine they're only too happy to have him playing somewhere else—and what he's doing with this group is a mystery.

And then it's my turn. I often treated the hole as a three-shotter because it was at the long end of my range and the water represented an unacceptable risk. But I pull out my driver, step behind the teed-up ball, make a relaxed practice swing and, peering down the fairway, park the Cutlass where I want it. I step up to the ball with a slightly closed stance, empty my mind of all thought except for my visualization, check my target precisely once, make a waggly little half swing, then turn my left shoulder to start the real McCoy. The ball leaves the tee in a high arc, launching down the middle of the fairway and drawing gently left, exactly as I intended. It sails through the open window 260 yards down, bounces another 20 yards or so and stops a few feet from the edge of the rough. "Onwards," I say. Then, to a chorus of "Nice ball," I pick up my carry bag and amble down the fairway.

Great start! Except that I barely reach full walking speed when I have to stop and wait as Cam, thankfully routineless, skids his ball another 140 yards in a vaguely appropriate direction. Then comes Dave, then Art, then Cam again, this time with an authentic hosel rocket. I briefly wonder if Cam has been planted in our group to push me over the mental health precipice the members know I have been clinging to. If so, foiled again. To my surprise, the psychological self-help retains its potency. Looking at about 215 yards to an easy pin, I pull out my 4-iron, perform the mind-calming rituals and pure a ball that lands softly near the front of the green and rolls to the back fringe, maybe 20 feet from the hole. "Wow," says Art. "Dude," says Dave.

And so it goes. Making like a judo black belt, I try to turn all of Cam's evil energy into something I can use to my own ends. This means striking up conversations with Art and Dave, a human impulse that I am usually immune to. In the case of the alien life form, my strategy is to follow the old laugh-with-not-at formula. Still, on the eighth green, when he not only sails his putt 15 feet past the hole but misses his line by 10, I can't resist the classic "How did that not go in?" to politely muted laughter from Art and Dave.

Not that Cam seems terribly concerned or even very sentient. By the time we all hole out on 9, he's staring at 60-something while Art and Dave have their predictable 39s and 40s. What no-one could have predicted is the 34 beside my name. "Wow," says Art. "Dude," says Dave. Cam is already in the snack bar stocking up on pastries.

A truly well person might be able to maintain his hard-won serenity through the entire round, but perhaps I am not yet that person because things do become mildly unglued on the challenging par-5 18th. I am sitting in the left rough 20 yards from the green after two, which leaves a difficult but not impossible up and down for a birdie. Dave is lying three on the fringe, Art has marked on the green, while Cam has managed to get his, I dunno, ninth shot to eight feet. At this point courtesy dictates that a golfer on the green walk to his ball, carefully checking to ensure he isn't treading on anyone's line, then mark the ball and dexterously pick a path to a spot where he is not in the line of vision of the next player up. Needless to say, he will then remain silent.

But Cam, he clomps across my line to mark his ball, then picks it up and clomps right back along the same track, probably grinding his size-12 shoes into the closely mown poa annua, the better to ensure my chip will not roll true. Then, about the time I have finished my preparatory swishes and am ready to address the ball, he decides that the spot he has chosen does not give him a sufficient view—or perhaps he just wants to be closer to his cart and its abundant food supply—so he walks back across my line to the opposite side of the green, where, well within my line of sight, he shifts into jingle-change mode and, incredibly, decides to start a conversation with Dave, who of course will have none of it, not a single "dude."

In my new and vastly improved psychological state, I vow that I will neither say anything to Cam nor allow him to affect my play. So much for that solemn pledge. First I chunk my chip, then I explode, "Jesus! Can you please be quiet." Even after thoroughly composing myself, I end up lipping out a four-footer for a bogey, the only blemish on my card and the reason I fail to break 70 for the first time in my life.

Still, I have sufficient perspective to see where on the scale of human adversity a score of two-under falls, and I am in a genuinely good mood as we retire to the bar to recount our round and await the arrival of the groups behind us. Almost 6,900 yards, with a rating of 72.8 and a slope of 132, Dunbar doesn't give up a lot of sub-par rounds, so much is made of my 70, especially as I haven't set foot on a course of any kind for a year. Indeed, as someone asks, where the hell did that come from?

"Well," I say, "did anyone notice my new swing?"

A couple of guys do think they spotted something different, which presents an entrée to talk up the great innovation. The idea of retaining much of the weight on the front foot inspires widespread incredulity, and someone asks if I'll step out to the range and demonstrate, which of course I do. Once they know what to look for, at least some of the guys can spot a couple of the subtle differences: the straight back leg, deeply dipped shoulder and exaggerated follow-through. And everyone can see the piercing flight of the balls I'm striking.

It's a command performance all around, and to keep it that way I leave the club after precisely two beers, just as I promised myself. Pulling away in the clattering Neon, I whistle like a farmer on his tractor heading out to the field. It's a wonderful thing, a simple song of contentment that would have become even more beautiful had it lasted more than six seconds. That's when I glance in the mirror at the car behind me, and my soaring heart sinks.

~ ~ ~ ~

MAY 1, FIVE DAYS EARLIER

They truly get it at the Tivoli Golf and Learning Center, the center of my existence and home instead of home. The generosity of the operating hours—from 5 a.m. till midnight, even on Christmas day. The condition of the balls—like they've just been shaken from a three-pack carton. The mats to hit from—as pristine as the wedding turf at a five-star hotel. But the capper has to be the constantly changing array of cars we are granted as targets. Seven of them, and color-coded for distance. Today at 150 yards, a fresh white 1976 Cutlass Supreme, replacing a white 1978 Cutlass Colonnade hardtop coupe, that itself replaced a white 1982 Cutlass Calais earlier in the year. A few weeks ago I was lured into conversation by the enthusiast on the next mat, and even took it upon myself to suggest that our steady diet of Oldsmobiles must have something to do with the wrecking yards being so full of them. "No," said the hacker. "These are all from the 1970s and 1980s, and most of those have been crushed. Big Bill spends good money on them because he hates Oldsmobiles so much, especially Cutlasses. He likes to hear the golf balls bouncing off of them, loves to watch the windows getting smashed."

Oh.

I knew that Bill Holm was the owner of the range, but not that he'd been a Saab dealer who went broke, as the guy explained. Beyond finding the Cutlasses intrinsically offensive, Holm blamed America's best-selling car for its role in enabling GM to buy the Swedish carmaker, then screw over his dealership. "That's his car in the parking lot," he said, gesturing toward a shiny black 900 convertible from the late 1980s. "The last model before GM got them."

Well, I kept an eye out for Big Bill after that, but I also keep my head down around here, with the result that I met him for the first time just yesterday. "It's Jeff, isn't it?" he said. "You've been putting in some serious time, Jeff. Must be working on something."

"Yeah."

"Crisp shots," he said. "And a different look. Where'd you pick up a swing like that?"

"Nowhere," I said. "It's all my own. I've been working on it for almost a year. You probably noticed."

"Uh-huh. A new swing takes work."

This was the longest conversation I'd had in several months, and it had pretty much exhausted me, but I was curious about

Bill, which is how I ended up walking back to his office. I don't know what I expected, but not a paean to Danish modern design from the 1960s, sparsely furnished with teak chairs and desk and low-slung pieces by designers like Hans Wegner and Arne Jacobsen, names that I remembered from another life. Settling into one of Jacobsen's Egg chairs, I tried for something articulate, along the lines of "Nice."

Bill agreed. His parents were Danes who opened a furniture store in the 1950s, he told me. He'd been seduced by all things Scandinavian, but from childhood his interests ran to the more conventionally male domains of autos and sport, and given Denmark's lack of prominence in these areas, he'd had to switch a big portion of his allegiance to Sweden. Thus, I deduced, the long ago Saab dealership, and also the neatly framed, signed photographs above a sleek Kaare Klint credenza: Annika Sorenstam, Henrik Stenson and Fredrik Jacobsen, plus a couple of Danish Sorens and Anders. I felt like I'd passed into a parallel universe where the game of golf is ruled over by svelte, blond technocrats with rarefied esthetic tastes and a tolerance for high levels of personal taxation. Basically, the precise opposite of the southern boys and country club kids who predominate on the PGA Tour, which really should consider changing its slogan from "These guys are good" to "These guys are Republicans."

Bill chatted about golf, and I pitched right in, sometimes with sentences of four words or more.

"So," he said, when it was time for me to go. "I hope you won't give up on that swing. The last really different one was Moe Norman's."

"Rings a bell," I responded.

"I should think," said Bill. "You've heard of Natural Golf."

"The funny, stiff-armed swing."

"Funny-looking, maybe, but effective. Moe Norman developed it, all on his own. It took him decades to get it right. Practiced the thing 12 hours a day. His hands would be bleeding."

I took care not to look down at the bandage on my right ring finger.

"He was easily good enough for the Tour, and he did play a few events, but he couldn't fit in. Some thought he wasn't quite right in the head."

I considered what some might think about my head.

"Tragic, really. He died a couple of years ago—in his 70s and he didn't have a cent."

My wallet pressed against my thigh, and it was a very light touch.

"Yeah," says Bill. "Apparently he was pretty much living in his car."

I didn't need to feel for my keys. The shitbox Neon I purchased to replace my company lease was in the shop again, and I spent an hour on the bus, with my clubs, getting to the range.

~ ~ ~ ~

It's time to make some changes. Forty-eight weeks. The therapist who diagnosed me with adjustment disorder said my case appeared to be a doozy, but the condition always dwindles away within a year. Well, I don't want to be the guy who makes them rewrite the psychiatry textbooks. And the classic way to start the first day of the rest of your life is by making a list.

Start dating
Terrifying, but it has to be done.

Look for job
Firmer ground, but what kind? Funnily enough, the boards I've been scanning don't indicate a lot of hunger locally for visioneers and placemakers. How sad that land developers should fail to see the competitive advantage offered by the guy who invents the back story that will then inspire the designers to turn

some chunk of nothingness into a cohesive development. How difficult for the marketers and salespeople who will have to sell condos and cul-de-sacs that have been insufficiently or even errantly themed.

Yes, a lot of mountain and golf resorts would be blander, less textured places if not for me. My big breakthrough was to specify that one or two structures had to be ungainly or even ugly, a way to deflect the common criticism that these kinds of developments are too much like amusement parks, that they, gosh, lack authenticity. Any old visioneer can figure out that the dusty corn field that's going to become a golf course subdivision was actually a fur trading post or some such thing. I went beyond that and specified a building that started life in the 1920s as a Hupmobile garage; in the 1930s was moved into by dust bowl refugees who tried to make it homey; by the 1940s had been abandoned to the pigeons because everyone was off to war; in the 1950s was expanded with a swoopy addition and turned into a dealership for Airstream travel trailers; by the 1970s was putting in time as a coffee shop and bingo hall, and in the 1990s was finally boarded up and then occupied by squatters who, incidentally, formed a band and put out an indie record that did OK in Japan.

At a company that took perverse pride in overthinking things, this was regarded as genius, an epochal breakthrough in the struggle to sell to hedge fund managers, cosmetic surgeons, district managers—the whole universe of real estate investors right down to the lower middle-income empty-nesters who floated down the river on a turd. They were loving it, all right, and sharing the love with a compensation package that not only grossed me $130,000 a year but paid my annual golf club dues, the provision being that I'd regularly host the various VPs and department heads who were years away from getting inside the gates at Dunbar, which is unequivocally the club to belong to in our fair burg.

And then, literally overnight, everything fell apart. Lighting someone's Porsche on fire is wrong. Yes, even if it's a Cayenne, even if its owner is one of those VPs, and even if he's been having sex with your wife.

I'm only aware too aware of my shortcomings, but the raging insanity took me by surprise. Some of it has to be chalked up to the unique set of circumstances, I think. So many events had to conspire, so many things had to go wrong.

First, our elegant and oh so environmentally sensitive push mower had to break down—and how many moving parts can there be?—meaning I had to pull out the old Toro, which in turn meant there was a can of gas sitting beside the front walk.

Two, the guys from the office had absolutely begged me to get them out on a Thursday afternoon, which would have been impossible except that the Thursday geezer group had an away game against another geezer group from the crap muni down the road—and how often is that egalitarian impulse going to be acted upon, even by old guys?

Three, the one guy I had much time for begged off after just one beer, meaning that I begged off after only three, back then another incongruity.

Four, Kevin Howell had to drive over and Fuck. My. Wife.

In retrospect, it's a good thing I'd had those beers. Because my judgment was impaired, my attorney was able to convince the crusading crime fighters they wouldn't get a conviction worth the time and effort. The drinking may even have helped with the severance settlement. It was almost a company outing, after all, and no-one at the office wanted to end up explaining the ritualized alcohol consumption in court. Also in my favor was the nature of my position, so specialized I'd never find another job like it. On the other side of the ledger, I'd been with the company for just six years, and, to be clear, I'd transformed the VP Marketing's sport-ubiquity-vehicle into a fireball that lit up the evening sky. At $100,000 the settlement wasn't unreasonable. No, that was left to the insurance company, which came after me for the price of the Cayenne. Maybe I'm being paranoid—me?—but I could almost hear the chuckling back in the executive suite when they got it.

So no, there won't be any visioneering jobs, not around here. And maybe, come to think of it, I'm getting ahead of myself even thinking about dating and a job search. Maybe, for now, there's room for only one thing on the list:

Resume human interactions

~ ~ ~ ~

MAY 2

At the range I make a point of seeking out Bill. As they say, baby steps.

In addition to being human, he obviously knows something of golf and is clearly an experienced business hand and all-round worldly guy. Seated once again in his office, I can't help but notice some paintings that escaped my notice yesterday when I was mesmerized by the furniture.

"Yeah," says Bill. "Denmark's best. My parents were into abstract expressionism, and I've been adding to the collection." The parallel universe continues to take on unexpected dimensions.

Bill is already onto the subject of golf instruction, and it dawns on me that he's considering whether I have something worth sharing. He watched me hit some balls and asked lots of perceptive questions. I explained the radical left-foot-weighting of my swing and all the little things I'd had to adjust to make it work. He seemed to both understand the thing and accept that it might be a winner. But does he have any insight into what I could do with it? "Well, first you have to make sure no-one else is teaching the same swing," Bill says. "If they are, you'll have to come up with a better name for yours."

Apparently the guy has done a little visioneering of his own. His fingers flying, Bill flicks from website to website, ticking off a list of teachers with similar approaches. Mac O'Grady, who won twice on Tour, doesn't seem to think people should keep as much weight on the left side; neither does Homer Kelley, author of a book called *The Golfing Machine*. Nor does another teacher of a similar ilk, Jim Hardy. "You know," says Bill. "I think you're onto something."

"So, now what?"

Then he utters three very beautiful words: "Want a partner?"

I think I play it pretty cool.

Back at the company I had a reputation as the world's worst negotiator. I was pretty much banned from dealing with anyone that mattered. Apparently, my flaw was an inability to understand what the other side wanted, or a lack of interest in calculating the likely consequences, or maybe just a propensity to cave. But I do OK with Bill, I think. It's not like I'm coming from a position of strength.

I have less than nothing to lose, so I just agree to everything he suggests. He and I will become 50/50 owners of the company that will market the swing. To this partnership I bring the swing and whatever portion of my time will be required by the enterprise. Bill will provide the teaching facility and office infrastructure and will bring to the relationship all of his golf-industry expertise and his many contacts, including several who aren't Scandinavian. As well, he'll pitch in the first $10,000 of capital, which will be used to produce marketing materials and such. He arrives at this figure by pulling up my account information. "In less than a year you've spent $9,995 on range balls," he says. "Incidentally, that's a record. Give me five bucks and we're good."

I hand over a fiver, and we shake hands.

Bill makes it clear what my immediate responsibilities are. Get back out on the course; post some low scores; enter some tournaments; gain some profile; talk up the swing; possibly work toward getting my PGA card. He refrains from saying anything along the lines of get your shit together, but I can read between the lines.

I am already onto it, in any case. In the morning, even before heading to the range, I called the club and told Ben in the pro shop I wanted to play in the Sunday morning Scratch Group. "Great to hear from you," he said. "Where have you been?"

"Around. Taking a bit of a vacation from golf."

"But you're coming back. That's terrific. Sure, there's a spot for you on Sunday. I'll tell the boys to get out their fire extinguishers."

I knew that's the way things would go, and briefly considered quitting the club, but what a stupid move that would have been, sentencing myself to a life of playing public courses. Maybe I should have taken a leave and saved myself thousands of dollars—except who expects to remain a mute hermit for 11 months?

"Funny, Ben, funny," I said. "Just do me a favor. Tell the guys I have a little surprise for them."

~ ~ ~ ~

JEFF, MAY 7

When the phone rings the morning after my triumphant return to the club, it takes me a couple of rings to figure out what's going on. In the weeks after I first moved into the apartment, there were phone calls from my attorney. But the legal issues ultimately shrank away, and it has been months since I've heard the distinctive tone.

"Hello." I say, quickly remembering the conventions associated with the device.

"Hi," responds the voice from afar, transmitted to my one-bedroom suite with balcony through the magic of 19th-century technology. "It's Ben. From Dunbar."

"Really," I say. "You've got some nerve."

"Why?"

"Let's talk about Cam Wallace for a minute. Is he really a member over at West Valley?"

"That's a question for the membership committee, not the pro shop, I'd say."

"Well, has this West Valley guy ever played at Dunbar before?"

"Never seen him."

"So, is there a chance he's not a West Valley guy but a rent-a-cop?"

"That's possible."

"It's not merely possible, it's probable. He was behind me in his rent-a-cop car as I was driving away. Together with that guy who was supposed to be an assistant. So, they were there to keep an eye on me?"

"That's possible."

"That's probable. And if I reached into my bag and pulled out a gun, their job was to shoot me?"

"You didn't have a gun in your bag."

"No, but you didn't know that."

"Yes, we did. We searched it."

"You searched my bag?"

"While you were getting a coffee. You said you had a surprise for us, and we were worried."

"What? Did you think I'm insane?"

"That's not why I called."

"Why did you call?"

"That left lean swing of yours. The members want lessons. Can I send Matt and Ross over to learn what it's all about?"

"Let me get this straight. First you arrange for greeters whose job is to shoot me, then you try to get your pros in on the ground floor so the members can pay you and not me?"

"Hey, that's not the way I look at it. I'm sending you your first two customers."

"Wow, yeah. OK, Ben—wait, can I get back to you?"

"Of course. Call me back this afternoon?"

"You got it!"

OK, so they were right. I'm not that brilliant a negotiator. The only thing that keeps me from selling the farm right there is the realization that I'm not in this alone. I have a partner, and on business matters such as this, it's imperative that I consult with him.

When I get down to the range, Bill is at his computer as usual. "What's new?" I say.

"You first," he replies, clicking off the screen and redirecting his attention toward me, exactly as a good partner should.

"Well, I went to the club yesterday. Shot a 70."

"Fantastic."

"Yeah, I showed them the swing. Now the head pro wants to send the two teaching pros for lessons."

"That's great."

"It is? I thought I should talk to you. I'm worried that letting the pros in is just going to cost us business."

"Don't fret too much. Two guys from the club already called and signed up for lessons straight from the master."

"Really!"

"A guy named James Chen wants to start on the weekend."

"Perfect. He'll love it."

"And another guy wants to come in today. I said 2 o'clock, OK? I signed him up for the six-lesson intro package. I put it through on his credit card. Our first $750." Bill reaches down to the floor and pulls up a tray with two glasses and a bottle of champagne on ice. "To the swing!"

How quickly a person's life can change. Less than a week earlier I was a barely recovering depressive with an infinitesimally tuned but entirely untested golf swing and future prospects as the world's oldest barista. Today I am the 50-percent owner of a fledgling business that shows every sign of success, the kind of guy that men respect and women admire.

"Hey Bill," I say as the first glass of mid-morning bubbly begins to kick in. "Do you date?"

"Are the Danes tall, smart and good looking?"

"In your case, absolutely. And with a strong chin and good hair too. But how does the dating thing work? I mean, you're 60."

"You don't think I can get it up?"

"No—I mean, yes! But where do you find the women? Bars? Some kind of service?"

"Craigslist."

"Does that really work? You don't need someone to screen them?"

"We're adults. We screen ourselves. We write our own ads. We put ourselves in the category we want to be in. We look at the category we want to look at."

"How do you mean, category?"

"On Craigslist if someone just wants sex, and the kinkier the better, it's Casual Encounters. Women Seeking Men and Men Seeking Women, they might be looking for sex or maybe just a date but probably a partner. Personally, I like Strictly Platonic."

"Why? If she's into Strictly Platonic, isn't she just looking for a friend?"

"Not always. Men and women together, that's a complicated thing. We're not really wired to be just friends, so it's only a matter of time before something happens. Women are perfectly aware of that, too, but they don't want to have to deal with horndogs."

"So what do you do?"

"Usually we go dancing. Every woman likes to dance. And when they dance…"

Bill gives me a sidelong glance just a couple of muscle clenches short of a wink, and I pretend I know what he's implying.

"So if I like her, I try to make the sale. If I don't like her or I can't make the sale, well, I still get to dance."

"How do you, uh, make the sale?"

"Apparently you forget, I spent 25 years selling cars; I owned a Saab dealership. You have to understand what the other person wants, you have to believe in your product, and you have to ask for the business."

"But doesn't that make you a … horndog?"

"Maybe it's our second or third time out. We have a lovely evening, we spend lots of my money, we dance till our feet are sore; after this, in awe of her beauty, drawn in by the force of such a magnetic personality, I am overcome with emotion and desire. Please, a gentleman such as this is not a horndog. A lady in this situation does not wish to remain just friends."

I realize I have so much to learn, and after so long I am ready to learn it. And not ready as in pathetic and needy, but ready as in eager and focused. I feel another whistling episode coming on. "Hey Bill. What's the name of the guy at 2?"

"Older fellow. Name is," he checks his trusty iMac: "Sam London."

CHAPTER 2
SYDNEY PARIS LONDON

JEFF, MAY 7, 2007

This is a dilemma of the first order. To the extent that such a thing is possible, I think that Sam always liked me. But there are complicating factors, his daughter being a seriously huge one.

Syd would be 37 this year, undoubtedly still lithe and athletic with sandy blonde hair, probably still fond of rust, orange and green, probably still neglectful of conventional underthings. Definitely still one of those rare left brain/right brain people who can be ultra-creative yet supremely practical at the same time.

How last century that we should have met as concerned citizens attending a municipal forum on neighborhood design controls. It seemed important at the time because I was finishing up a masters degree in urban planning intended to set me on the kind of career path my undergrad degree in cultural studies had so convincingly failed to. At 26 Syd—the full name would be, yes, Sydney Paris London—was already an architect, and a good one. Between school and interning it takes eight years even to hang out one's shingle, and here she was a junior partner in a small firm that all the right people were talking about, not that I was one of them or knew anything about anything.

At issue was the desire of almost everyone who lived in Syd's leafy neighborhood to prevent incoming plutocrats from knocking down their mock Tudors so they could be replaced with mock Mediterranean villas. I can only speculate on their motives. Many no doubt had a deep affection for the area, an early 20th-century streetcar suburb that had turned into an inner-city sanctum of comfortable but not extravagant houses on big garden lots. A few were perhaps more concerned with the ethnic makeup and thought that newcomers from Asia and the Middle East might avoid the area if moving there meant putting up with half-timbering and rose gardens. I was there because I was writing my thesis on development conflicts in established neighborhoods and I wanted to see how the plucky residents made out in their fight against rapacious developers and heritage-defiling philistines.

Some of these history-razers and lot-rapists were in attendance, but sensing the mood in the room, they kept their thoughts to themselves. Even the consultants hired to deliver a carefully crafted message of compromise and consultation were unable to dent the wall of stony hostility. It seemed the neighborhood would remain forevermore a rare west coast outlier of Medieval manse architecture. And then up stood a young woman who could only be described as breathtaking. Introducing herself as a resident and architect, she neatly summarized everyone's concerns and then explained why the preferred solution would be not only ineffective but ultimately damaging. Strict design controls would freeze the natural course of architecture, she said, preventing it from reflecting the technology of the day and the constantly evolving way that people live their lives. The kind of Revival Revival homes that resulted would amount to a simple case of elevating style over substance. If people were truly looking for the feel of an English or European neighborhood, they should do what the Europeans do: Build homes to last for centuries, insist on higher standards for architects, builders and tradespeople, and inculcate a high degree of design literacy in the populace.

She sat down, and the consultants instantly stood up and began to speak, suddenly remembering the message they were being paid to deliver. More importantly, there was an audible buzz as residents began talking among themselves, soul searching, wondering of spouses and neighbors if their motives had been above reproach. Those lawyers, doctors, professors and brokers began to behave like Shakers worried they'd harbored impure thoughts.

Or so I imagined, possibly because of the impure thoughts I was harboring myself. One would never guess this of a future visioneer, but I am shy with women, partly because I'm just shy with women, partly because I'm inclined to look upon things from the viewpoint of a detached observer, and as a detached observer I could see what might be in a relationship for me, I just couldn't see what might be in it for the woman.

That put me in a position of stammering weakness when I somehow got up the courage to go over and introduce myself to Ms. London. Which, as it turned out, was not a bad position to be in.

Our courtship can best be described as whirlwind. Getting drunk and hooking up has achieved cultural currency in recent years, but the concept was already familiar back in 1996. A week later I moved in with her. The situation was all but incomprehensible, and yet Syd's judgment of me and my prospects proved to be fairly sound. Upon graduating I quickly found a job working with a suburban planning commission, and we fell comfortably into the surprisingly clichéd existence of young urban professionals, a style of life previously familiar to me only from bad 1980s movies, as if in the '80s there were any other kind.

This world included golf, a recreational activity I'd believed to be the strict domain of mutton-chopped Scots and dissolute salesmen, as well as the elderly and infirm. I was quickly assured this was not the case—that golf is in fact a demanding sport. And yet, it seemed to be my destiny to prove the contention wrong. My first time at the club it was assumed I'd provide a measure of comic relief, even though Syd's father, Sam, a six-time club champion, undertook to provide a modicum of instruction. A true student of the game, he tried to get me going on what I've since learned is called the modern swing. Until the last couple of decades, players like Jack Nicklaus and Johnny Miller turned their hips quite a bit on the backswing, kept their heads behind the ball and generated a lot of their power using bent knees that helped propel the club through impact. With the modern swing, golfers try to minimize knee flex and lateral movement, shifting their weight but not their body, and using the rotation of the hips around their rigid left side to generate power.

Embarrassing that I should care about such things when children in Botswana are going hungry, but what can you do? As much as Sam and Syd seemed to love the game, I seemed to love it more. They didn't adore the look of my swing, which was on the quick side and involved a bit of unfashionable lower body action, but they couldn't help but be impressed by the results. The first time out Syd suggested I play from the forward tees so as not to slow the course or provoke disillusionment, and wouldn't you know it, I outdrove her on every hole, typically by 60 or 70 yards. My third time out I broke 100 from the white tees and by the end of the year I'd shot a 90 from the tips. In the darkest-before-dawn days of the pre-Tiger golf recession, I was able to join the club for the princely sum of $12,000, $43,000 less than it would cost me today.

You had to love the 20th century. We'd golf two or three times a week and have sex twice that often. And we were equally compatible when not putting the pole in the hole, as our dual-purpose description went. She was a less introverted loner, I was a more introverted loner, and each of us was content to spend time alone, together, or alone together.

To the extent that we needed contact with other people, there was also the thing called work. In my case it was months before I got over the thrill of not having to don a green apron and pull someone a latte. Then for the next couple of years, there was enough to absorb that the surprisingly tedious nature of my tasks hardly mattered. Looking at the profession from the outside, I'd assumed my career would involve sketching out grand boulevards and founding sustainable new towns with centralized solar heating. The reality is that a planner drafts rules, coaches elected officials into enacting them, then spends most of his hours ensuring they're enforced. And that's the majordomos, such as they are. For juniors like me the daily grind was mostly about helping developers get their rubber stamp, punctuated now and then with more intriguing stuff, like determining the cost of provisioning handicap bus service in semi-rural areas.

As the years passed my dull and rules-bound existence was thrown into even starker relief by Syd's ever more brilliant career. She'd arrived on the scene at precisely the right time, a moment when virtually her entire profession realized that with the aberration known as postmodernism they'd committed a crime against the people and needed to be sent to a Maoist re-education camp, if not indeed executed. But Syd was untainted. She had never worked on a building the color of a child's toy or tarted up with classical embellishments. And if postmodernism was bad, Syd not only knew what was good, she could produce it. She called herself a Modernist, and never neglected to capitalize the "M." Indeed, she uttered the words Alvar Aalto—which, as we were prone to point out, is not an incantation from a Harry Potter book but the name of a mid-20th century Finnish architect— with the reverence other women reserved for the manufacturers of fancy pumps. But Syd also believed that architecture could not ignore the march of technology, and to her that meant exploiting the potential of contemporary building materials and techniques. Equally important, she insisted that the computer programs architects were beginning to employ weren't just time-saving tools but, if I may quote her, integral inputs that could and should be reflected in every completed structure.

She was hardly alone in the CadCam camp. But where an architect like Frank Gehry emphasized the decorative possibilities, Syd and her office remained true to the modernist creed that form follows function. And the approach seemed to work. The progressively more important buildings originating with the firm tended to jolt people at first glance but quickly settled into the cityscape, where they took on an aura of grace and timelessness without ever losing a certain subtle wow factor.

It's not easy being a schlub and living with a woman you recognize to be a celestial star. If I may be allowed a moment of self-pity, it's even harder when the rest of the world begins to realize it too. Fortunately, just as Syd and her firm were making the leap from doughty local alt-heroes to international up and comers, I was taking a little flea-hop of my own.

Let's be clear, I am genuinely not a people person. And yet I do like to drink. No-one wants to drink on their own, and even if they do—and this is an important distinction—they don't want to be someone who drinks alone.

So I drank with other primates. Since I had no real pals, and Syd was increasingly traveling or busy at work, this usually meant my co-workers and their friends. The group was heavily weighted toward those in our own and related professions, so it wasn't long before I knew a lot of relevant people, including some who were under the impression that I was an intelligent and potentially able fellow, even someone who seemed vaguely likable.

Without even trying to I was networking, and networking, as everyone knows, is the key to career success. It probably didn't hurt that I was living with an architect widely recognized as being the hottest in town—and also the most rapidly ascending, if you catch my drift. Anyway, it wasn't long before one of these bar pals asked if I was interested in interviewing for a job at his company.

I believe this person's name was—yes, that's it; his name was Kevin Howell.

Well, who knows what Kevin was up to? I'm definitely not the person to decide, what with the gut-clenching bitterness, the jealous rage and all. But let it be said that if I wasn't hired because I was the best person for the job, I certainly proved that judgment to be in error. Within months I'd been promoted to a more senior position, which I quickly transformed into my pioneering visioneer gig. Believe what one will about such an indefensible role, I made the most of it. Someone steeped in cultural studies might suggest I'd been contributing more to society minding suburban zoning bylaws for less than half the salary, but that person didn't get to sketch out a grand boulevard or decide that a neighborhood in a ski resort would get, yes, centralized solar heating. Sure, we put it there to generate publicity and appeal to the target demo of lesbian snowboarders making even more money than we were, but still. And even if it didn't contribute all that much to the march of human progress, that little triumph and others like it definitely enhanced my own feelings of self-worth, which in turn altered the previously lopsided dynamic between Syd and me, which in turn led me to propose to her.

And no, this did not proceed smoothly. I honestly believe that Kevin was not yet poking into places he didn't belong. I think it had more to do with my ham-handed performance. Irony has its place, and perhaps this was not one of them, even with Syd. Maybe there's a reason why, when men elect not to go the quietly romantic route, they're likely to opt for something that strikes them as quirkily extravagant. The billboard or Jumbotron-type gambit, say. Everyone will think them retarded, but it's likely that she's similarly dim, and the episode will give them something to reflect upon later in life. I opted instead for the more quietly idiotic approach of dropping onto one knee in exaggerated fashion and saying, in what I took to be a send up of courtliness but might have come across as a mockery of true love and devotion, "Sydney Paris London, I request your hand in marriage."

Syd did her best to manage the situation, of course. She displayed genuine emotion, exactly as I wish I had done. But she did not say yes. Instead, she said she would have to think about it. She was flattered but also taken aback, or words to that effect. In retrospect this was a perfectly reasonable reaction. Why has our culture elevated the out-of-the-blue proposal, anyway? Probably because reproduction would suffer a steep decline if women came to believe they had a moment to think it over. But I was beyond rational consideration. The terror of popping the question had been replaced by the horror of rejection. The blood that generally races to my penis when in Syd's presence instead streamed to my head, to the detriment of both. Everything went blank, and I just stood there, or rather knelt.

"I think we could use a drink," Syd finally said. I stood up and brushed off my knee. We poured some wine and began to make conversation, which was not even excruciating. It didn't take long for my blood flow resume its normal pattern and not much longer for us to jump into bed. A half hour or so of not resting apparently gave Syd the time she needed to think, because she soon allowed that she would be thrilled to marry me. God, I loved that woman.

Well, we had our wedding: a civil ceremony in her parents' back yard, two dozen guests, five-day honeymoon at a lodge in the Rockies because Syd was so busy. Not much changed afterwards except that Kevin Howell took a shine to our hot tub. Irony, indeed.

~ ~ ~ ~

Waiting for Sam to appear, I can't avoid the reality that the Syd issue, massive though it is, will not be the only elephant in the stall. I mean, given all the hours Sam put into teaching me the game, can I now turn around and charge him to do likewise? It probably won't bother him to spend the money, because certainly he can afford it, so I am able to make an executive decision that I hope will seem appropriate to both Sam and Bill. Just like in the heroin business, the first one will be free. If Sam wants to cut things off there, he'll get his money back. If not, we'll give him a discounted rate.

So, fine. But another thing may not be so easy to resolve. It would seem that around the time of the Porsche incident and the Kevin Howell break-in—in fact, just as the pale light of dawn was breaking on the same cursed night—there had been another strange occurrence. Someone had roto-tilled the words "FUCK YOU TOO SYD" into Sam and Georgia's front lawn. This could not have been me because, as I pointed out to the authorities, I am something of a grammarian and would not have omitted the necessary comma between "too" and "Syd." For some reason this angered the gumshoes, who nevertheless speculated that it had been me, and that I perpetrated the act because Syd's and my house was under police observation, whereas Sam and Georgia were out of town. In any case the lawn took several months to repair itself, and during this time became something of a local attraction. One could not be certain how Sam might feel about this.

So, yes, I am nervous when Sam arrives, sharp at 2. My apprehensions dissolve when he walks up to me, all 6'1" of him, grabs me around the shoulders and gives me a big hug. "God, it's good to see you," he says. "Georgia and I missed you so much. Why didn't you call? Why didn't you answer your phone?"

I melt, of course. Sam has a way of saying this that doesn't even sound accusatory, just one of the many gifts enjoyed by a guy who started out superhuman and has gotten better with age. Man, even his backstory is a case of pure visioneering genius: a poor farm boy who'd known the country was no place for a guy like him and hit the road the day he graduated from high school, spending the subsequent three or four years living a life straight out of the vintage *Route 66* television series, working and adventuring up and down the coast with epic detours into and across the mountains, and all this while driving an MGA. In 1962, when he would have been 21, he decided to go to college, leaving four years later with a degree in engineering.

He never sought his professional designation, though, because he never had to. While in fourth year he worked part-time at a factory and hit upon a minor technical improvement that he thought might be patentable. Ultimately his tiny tweak proved to be too similar to someone else's, but the process opened his eyes to the immense storehouse of unexploited ideas and innovations that is the patent office. His first coup involved picking up the rights to a semi-automated deep-frying system that hadn't panned out back in 1936 but proved to be just the thing in 1965, as America headed down the road to becoming the world's first fast-food nation. Next he found a forgotten 1908 gadget designed to prevent pilferage of industrial pulleys, a problem that apparently died out in 1909, only to resurface in the 1960s when the role of the pulleys was taken by the expensive mag wheels easily stolen from parked muscle cars by the decade's exploding population of miscreants. He would go on to pick up many such patents, some useless, others world-changing in their own minuscule way, but in the meantime he also came across Georgia.

As photographs, historical accounts and my own observation three decades later make clear, she was quite the find. A child of bohemia and a grad student at Berkeley, Georgia was living across the bay in the Haight in 1966, the year that she and Sam met. The neighborhood was only a year away from becoming the nexus of the hippie nation, but Georgia was ahead of even that curve. Among other things, she was working on short stories falling into a genre that wouldn't even exist for another generation, when it would come to be known as feminist erotica. She called her sex-drenched yet warmly humanistic tales "cliterature," but as often seemed to be the case with Georgia, the world was not quite ready for what she had to give it and she couldn't find a real publisher.

Why the couple left the Bay Area for our backwater burg after Syd was born in 1970 is not completely clear to me. It wasn't a pure case of suburban flight, and Sam the farm boy certainly knew better than to head back to the land. Still, in their own way the young couple with their babe in arms might have been participating in the unusual urban diaspora that characterized the times. Not that they subjected themselves to any sort of deprivation. Sam's allegiance lay more with the generation that produced optimistic types—your Bobby Darins and Sammy Davis Jrs.—than with the protesters and drug takers that followed. With a nice income flowing in from the deep-fryer and wheel locks, they purchased a house designed by a colleague of Richard Neutra in a neighborhood conveniently adjacent Dunbar Gates, which Sam immediately joined. Georgia largely abandoned writing in favor of painting and photography, soon becoming known for her nudes.

Meanwhile, Sam kept turning up patent after patent with overlooked commercial potential even if, alas, there were no more runaway winners. Typically his gizmos worked well enough but ran up against competition that did likewise, meaning that Sam had to become more of a marketer, which wasn't a stretch for him but did force him to spend a good deal of time on the road, often far afield. I actually accompanied him on one of these trips, during the year between moving in with Syd and scoring my big career break as a guardian of suburban zoning bylaws.

Back then I had a vague proficiency in Spanish, a remnant of two months spent in central America, when my 21-year-old self had thought of himself as the questing type. Sam was peddling some proprietary technology originally intended for Vietnam-era military communication but suddenly of use to self-serve gas stations, which were just beginning to debut in areas outside the

First World. He had already traipsed alongside his competitors through Argentina, Chile and many of the former Iron Curtain countries, and now he saw a similar opportunity in the poorer reaches of South America. On his trip to Lima I would save him the expense of hiring a local interpreter.

Well, what a rare and inexcusable gaffe on his part. It's possible Sam was blinded by my surprising competence at golf, or maybe he just wanted to get the measure of the unlikely fellow his cherished daughter had inexplicably fallen for and was willing to pay the price. But, really. To begin he expected me to drive, an experiment that lasted all of a half-hour. In Lima there are only two ways to go: the paranoid, halting approach of crawling along the curb. Or the favored local method of keeping one hand on the horn, the other on the gearshift, and making like a sperm attempting to beat all others to the ultimate goal. I was restricted to the first, of course, and we'd made it only a couple of miles from the airport when the banditos struck. Anyone with half a brain and a similar quotient of balls would have thrown the car into reverse and screeched away when the truck carrying two men with automatic rifles swerved in front of us and hit the brakes. With Sam yelling frantically in my ear to Drive! Drive! Drive! I rolled down the window to inquire, "*Que pasa, amigo?*"

They stole everything. Sam took it in stride even as I, still quivering, indulged in an orgy of self-recrimination. Three days later, when sufficient supplies had arrived from home and a car and driver had been duly hired, I proved to be virtually useless as an assistant. This was not so much due to my Spanish, but to my inability to pick up on what the two sides were really trying to say to each other. Apparently, I'm unable to even *translate* a negotiation.

And yet Sam couldn't have been less bothered. Despite my help he managed to sell enough of his electronic doodads to pay for the trip, which he told me had been a real treat and a true adventure. I mean, where do people like him come from?

Now his sweetness and decency is in evidence all over again. Everyone but everyone at the club is buzzing about my new swing, he says. He wants to be the first one in because his game is beginning to desert him and he's desperate for something that might help. "Not sure if you've talked with Syd lately," he says, a little disingenuously. "But she's been playing a lot. A lot. Last time she gave me two strokes and still won. Shot a damn 71."

"Really?" I say. Pathetically, I still want to hear about Syd, and equally pathetically, I want to hear about her golf game.

"Yeah, playing a lot of golf," he says, denying me further details. "But why the hell am I suddenly a six? Sixty-six isn't that old. Help!"

This is the first lesson I've given, and I've planned my approach, but first I want to make sure that everything is cool between Sam and me. "Help is on the way," I say. "But before I start the meter there are a couple of things I want to discuss with you."

Sam is almost indignant when I launch into the money talk, adamant that he will pay full freight. This does not surprise me, but his reaction when I bring up the lawn episode does. "Georgia and I thought that was the funniest thing we'd ever seen," he laughs. "We were very sad about the two of you, understand. But the lawn was priceless. And it's been great for Georgia."

"*Really?*"

"I was going to till the area and fix it up with some new turf. Could have done it by the end of the day. But Georgia decided she wanted to document it, and after she'd videoed it and taken some shots, she asked me to leave it for a couple of days. She wanted to see what happened as the grass grew and the script subtly changed. Well, we left it for a year."

"I noticed," I say. "I think other people did, too."

"Yeah, hilarious," he says. "Delegations of concerned parents worried that their children would read the word 'fuck.'"

"Anything for art."

"You don't know the half of it," he says. "Georgia started playing around with the clips, and decided she wanted some more. We ended up renting a vacant place with a big lawn and tilling in all kinds of phrases. She shot them the same way, week after week, and edited it all together into a 10-minute clip."

"What for?"

"At first, no real reason, just something that people like her do. But I've got a hydroponics patent just now—the marijuana business is huge, you know—and she started thinking about that. She asked me if I could build her an installation with grass. And damned if she doesn't have a show starting next month back in San Francisco! You'll walk inside this dark room, the clip with all these somehow meaningful phrases will be playing, and you'll gradually realize you're surrounded by lawn, which is of course growing. There's another phrase embedded in the grass, which will gradually be revealed as the show progresses, and there's a camera trained on that, so you'll be able to see it all in time lapse on another screen. Strange, hey? All those years of writing and painting, and no-one really seemed to get it. Finally, the big break, and it's all about watching grass grow!"

Sam is pretty chuffed, and I can't blame him. This is not the time to bring up the quasi-suicidal thoughts I've entertained on my regular detours by a spot I've come to view as a monument to my casting from paradise. "Glad to be of assistance," I say, with what I hope is the appropriate sardonic tone. "Now, let's see if we can reinvigorate someone else's career."

I watch Sam hit a few shots and I think I can see what is happening to his game. Always a big hitter, he can't bear to lose distance as his strength and flexibility gradually ebb, and without really realizing it he's started to exaggerate his weight shift to get those extra yards. He is even lifting his left heel a touch, as older players tend to do. All that extra movement is turning him into the same kind of player I'd been: an inconsistent ball striker. This is going to be easy.

"OK," I say. "Let's try something." Unlike most teachers, who start out their students with short irons, I get Sam to pull out his driver. The thing with my swing is that you're able to use your front leg as a kind of axle more freely with the driver, so it's easier to pick up the feeling of what you should be doing while swinging the big stick.

Sure enough, after 10 or 12 progressively less awkward swings, Sam hits a powerful draw that plows into a rare yellow Oldsmobile parked against the fence 250 yards away, producing a most satisfying ding. "Wow," he says. "Haven't hit one like that in five years."

A half-hour later he is hitting crisp iron shots, too. There is still work to be done, and Sam is going to have a hard time remembering and repeating everything he's picked up, but the point is, in an hour-long lesson he has changed his swing considerably and yet is hitting the ball better than he has in years.

"Man, I should be paying you," I tell him. "Thank you for being the ideal student."

"Don't mention it," he says in his own attempt at a sardonic tone. "See you in the club championship."

~ ~ ~ ~

As I walk Sam to his car, that innocent remark bothers me. Sure, he is a prince of a man, but will he now go back and tell all his pals about this fantastic swing I am teaching? Or, with visions of a miraculous seventh club championship dancing in his head, will he horde it all for himself? And what about me? Am I doing the right thing? Would I not be better off to keep my historic breakthrough to myself, take a job as Bill's ball picker, hit 15 buckets a day and play it cool till the Champion's Tour beckons in a mere 12 years?

When I get back to the little office Bill has set up for me, there is a surprise. Before Sam's arrival I had a few moments to check out Craigslist, and even took a stab at posting an ad of my own. And now, waiting for me, is a response. "I'm intrigued. Free golf lesson, no strings attached? Count me in. I'm 32 and separated. I think of myself as easy going. Other people say I'm easy on the eyes. Fore!"

Not a bad start. Still, I have to ask myself if am I ready for this. Ready for a dating scene that can only be bizarre? Ready to trade down to what will probably be a Neon, or at best one of Bill's oddball Saabs, after 11 years of driving an Aston-Martin?

Damn right, I'm ready. It has been 10 months since I've even spoken to a woman who wasn't wearing a police uniform and clarifying the terms of a court order.

"Hello."

"Uh, hi. It's Jeff. Golf guy."

"Wow. That was quick."

Too quick. Damn. "Well, I'm desperate."

Pause. "My name is Jenny, but I did find your post under Strictly Platonic, right?"

Damn, again. "Right. A little confused. Trying to be funny."

She actually laughs a touch. "OK, sorry. I'm not really that uptight. Just new to this."

"Me, too."

"But you really will give me a golf lesson?"

"Absolutely."

"So you're a pro?"

"Not a pro, a teacher."

"How does that work?"

"I haven't gone through the process that would get me into the PGA. But otherwise it's not that different. I'm based at a driving range, the same as a lot of pros." No need to mention that the arrangement is all of three days old.

"OK. So, you want to set something up?"

"Sure. Any time."

"Well, how about, oh, now?"

"Let me check my diary. Yes, now seems to be clear."

You have to love Craigslist. Three hours after my first post, I am shaking Jenny's soft, warm hand, willing my eyes to stay trained well above her curvy, cashmere-covered chest, and cursing myself for going with Strictly Platonic. But I promised a golf lesson, and dammit, she's going to get a golf lesson. I have never instructed anyone other than a six-time club champion, but she's only interested because she's inherited an aunt's old Wilsons, so what does she know?

With only an hour to work with, I want to get her out there with club in hand as quickly as possible. Grip: check. Stance: check. Alignment: check. Now eyes on the ball, stick that ass out, mind the wrist cock, point that shoulder to the ground and be sure to follow through. And here we go, despite the mass of information swirling in your brain and the overwhelming fear of looking like an idiot, relax every muscle in your body and let's try a swing. And yes, that would be my swing rather than the standard one.

Well, she does OK, and I think I do too. We spend a solid hour on the range, and she's clearly feeling some fatigue, but I can tell she doesn't want to quit. "Want to try the putting green?" I ask.

"But my hour is up," she objects.

"I have nothing but time."

"Why is that?" she asks.

"Long story."

"I'll tell you mine if you tell me yours," she says.

This is going well. We are alone on the green, so we chat about ourselves between my occasional putting tips. She's a journalist type who was married to a computer type before things turned sufficiently sour or became sufficiently dull that they decided, as other adults apparently do, to calmly go their separate ways. In turn I relate my story, edited for brevity, clarity and naked self-interest. "Hey," I eventually say, without hardly agonizing over it.

"I'd be happy to give you another lesson some time. But if there's something else platonic you'd like to do in the meantime, I'm up for that too. For example, you don't eat food and drink alcohol, do you?"

"Only platonic alcohol."

"So that would be ouzo and retsina?"

Perhaps enjoying our little joke too much, we go to a Greek restaurant, order dalmathes and calamari and wash these down with pinesap-tainted wine, followed by shots of licorice liqueur to go with our baklava. After doing this, we tell each other we've had a wonderful time, demurely kiss goodnight and agree to reconnect in a couple of days. Could the mingling and perhaps mating of men and women really be so easy?

When I get back to the apartment there is a message waiting. A female voice: "Hey Jeff. Give me a call."

The voice is Syd's.

~ ~ ~ ~

MAY 8

There is something for me to see this morning at Bill's House of Denmark. But first I have something for Bill—a tray of Danishes.

"Your cultural heritage," I offer.

"Not really."

"What do you mean by that?"

"Danishes are actually Viennese. Not healthy enough for us. There was a bakers' strike in the 19th century, and the owners brought in foreign bakers. One thing led to another."

"Yeah, well, we don't call them Austrian pastries."

"It's just an Americanism. A Danish guy opened a bakery in New York. Something to do with a President being in love with the things. An accident of history."

Impressive, if a little surprising, to see Bill so humble about yet another Danish contribution to modern living. "Hey, I've never been to Denmark, but everything I hear is so positive."

"What do you hear?"

"Well, this is kind of weird, but my mom is also a Dane-ophile, if that's the right word. She went there first for a scientific conference and liked it so much she vacationed there a couple of times. Even moved to Copenhagen for a few months during a sabbatical."

"Clearly your mom is a woman of taste and breeding," says Bill.

Well, Bill, if only you knew. But no need to broach the topic of my mom. If the business relationship endures, he will find out more about her than he could possibly want. "Clearly," I say.

"I haven't shown this to a lot of people, but I'm planning to update the driving range," says Bill, changing the subject. With his abundant social graces, he recognizes that, for all of Denmark's ultra-specialness, I have already talked enough about a place that I've never been to. "Interested in looking at the drawings?"

"Love to," I say. "It used to be an important part of my job. Sometimes I even got to be the prick that sent them back to the drawing board."

I realize this remark sounds like something from another kind of person, someone decisive and inclined to take charge, someone with a positive self-image. In fairness to myself the de-signers and architects loved liaising with me because they knew they could talk me into almost anything. Sometimes it caused them grief farther up the line when I couldn't sell the higher ups on their more outré ideas, but it can't be denied that I developed a reputation as a guy who got the best out of them. Maybe it was because I absorbed something through Syd. Or maybe it actually makes sense to respect creative people, and to give them as much freedom and scope as possible.

"So," says Bill. "I have a friend who teaches at the architecture school. Finnish guy." In Bill's world, the Finns are pretty close to the Danes, regardless of how strangely they may speak. Although they can't seem to golf or build cars like the Swedes, they can live in a functional and stylish manner, and design things, which puts them well ahead of the sadsack Norwegians, who disappoint in almost all of these important areas.

"He recommended a recent graduate who'd draw something up cheap, for the experience. Things aren't so hot for architects these days, you know."

"Really?"

"That's what I hear,"

"Right." Maybe something has changed during my Rip Van Winkle year, but I can't imagine what.

"Jussi says he's the next Rem Koolhaus." This is a name that would mean as much to most golfers as would Butch Harmon to most non-golfers. But Bill and I bonded over our shared knowledge of which is the celebrity swing coach and which is the avant-garde Dutchman. I also understand Bill's point of view that the Dutch, while not technically Scandinavian, have a kind of honorary status due to their similar esthetic sensibilities, even if they do tend to be a little too chatty.

"So, what do you think?"

"Wow."

"Yeah, I know," says Bill.

Bill's young architect has tapped into a trend sometimes called biomimicry, which intrigued Syd as well. For a big competition in L.A., her firm partnered with a firm there and submitted an amazing, undulating structure that heaved and rolled like some sort of sea monster around the perimeter of the oceanside site, leaving the center for a kind of strange, seaweedy garden. It responded to all the program needs of the client, looked great and added a lot of additional features. The day they learned the job had gone to someone else, she came home and said, "Let's get drunk," a request I was happy to comply with. As it happened, the big national firm that won the thing had a crappy branch office in a suburban business park located conveniently nearby and, equally conveniently, adjacent a lightly used park. Juvenile to say the least, but late that evening we drove out there with a shag bag and, from a well-concealed spot, shot 3-woods at the wall of windows, hitting it with almost every swing. Fortunately, a golf ball has expended most of its energy by the time it's ready to land, so nothing broke. That's why Tiger or Phil can sail a 300-yard drive into the gallery and everyone will be fine, but let a hacker shank his pathetic 6-iron into a buddy standing off to the side, and it's stretcher time.

Bill's young architect came up with a strange humpy shape for the building to house Bill's new office, which will have to be about twice as big to make room for lots of launch monitors and such, not to mention office space for our little enterprise. The size of the property is a serious constraint for Bill. There are already days when every parking spot is taken, and the really big hitters are starting to knock the occasional ball over the back netting, 255 yards away. He'd asked the architect to consider this, maybe find a way to add 10 yards to the hitting area or put in some underground parking, if it wasn't too expensive. The designer opted for a very different solution, taking away Bill's short game area, with its space-eating bunkers and chipping green, and putting it instead on the living, eco-approved roof, it of the humps and bumps. From the road the new building will look like nothing so much as a Scottish links course, with fescues waving in the wind. Only after you drive in will you see that the grassed-over dunes conceal a building—a very sleek and modern building that would look right at home in Denmark—and that people are practicing on top of it. "I got my extra 10 yards, my energy costs will be lower, and the roof will absorb enough rainwater that I won't have to spend money on a new drainage system," says Bill.

Brilliant all around. "It has to cost more, though," I say, the only objection I can muster.

"Not if you consider the extra parking spots," says Bill. "Thirty more spaces without having to go underground or buy the lot next door."

"Contemporary architecture strikes again," I say, taking care not to mention the phone message from the contemporary architect I am most familiar with. Bill and I discussed my situation with Syd, and I am aware of his take on relationships turned toxic—that there are an infinite number of fish in the sea, so it's stupid to waste one's time on a blowfish, regardless how delicious, when it has the potential to kill you.

But it is time to head out to the range to meet Ross, from the club, an encounter I am not looking forward to—and for good reason, as it turns out. He's always been a classic jock, with the barest tolerance for Johnny-come-lately, vaguely artistic types like me. Twenty minutes in, he tells me the swing is a crock of shit and hack amateurs shouldn't be teaching anyway, not when there are real pros with families to feed. With that he picks up his clubs and departs, leaving me to work on a hitch that has developed in my own swing, one that causes me every now and then to, god forbid, hit a hosel rocket.

I don't get home till 9 that night, and minutes after I walk in the door, the phone rings.

"Hello."

"Hi, Jeff."

"Syd."

"I knew you wouldn't call me."

"I would have. I haven't had time."

"You wouldn't have."

"I would have. Everything is different now."

"Everything?"

"Everything."

"Then there's no reason you can't go golfing with me, is there?"

"Uh…"

"I've been playing a lot. Down to a five now. You won't even have to give me a stroke, if that's the problem."

"Uh."

"The restraining order has expired, if that's what you're worried about."

"Uh…"

"I called your range and booked a lesson for Thursday at 5—which I'm hereby canceling. You're now free, if that's why you're hesitating.

"Uh."

"We'll just play nine holes, if stamina's the issue."

"Uh."

"Can I take that as a yes? I've got a tee time at 5:40. Front nine."

"Uh…"

"Just say yes."

"Do you really think this is a good idea?"

"Is everything different?"

"Everything is different."

"Then it's a good idea."

"All right, then. Be sure to let Ben know. He'll want to put some snipers in the trees.

~ ~ ~ ~

MAY 9

Another Jeff Jones negotiation. She wants to get together and play golf. I don't. We will be getting together and playing golf.

And why don't I? Any man would want to see Syd, let alone an ex who has tried but failed to extinguish the flame. But is everything really different? Am I really so thoroughly healed? After all that's happened, can we now exist as fellow club members and even friends the way that Jenny and her ex apparently do? I wish I had more confidence.

"Any words from the wise, Bill?" I try. It isn't easy for a man to ask another man for advice, so I feel that just doing so is a demonstration of the mental health I now possess and will absolutely need. "I'm going to see Syd again this evening. First time in 11 months. We're going to golf nine at the club."

"Jesus," he replies. "Your idea?"

"No, hers."

"You think she's still with the other guy?"

"Dunno."

"Like to help, but there are too many variables. Don't want to steer you wrong. Jesus, be careful."

"Er, thanks." That's a sobering exchange, and not at all what I was expecting. I've never seen Bill without an instant take on a situation, particularly one that involves the care and feeding of women. Moreover, it's his role to play the confidence-inspiring backslapper, to say "Hey, big guy, you're the man." Can it be that my apprehension is justified?

But it's time to take my insecurity from the office to the range. In three days of giving lessons, I've learned a lot. Bill and I have decided that for $750 students should get the full package, including video and launch monitor records of their entry and exit swings, so I've had to become proficient at those functions. More challenging is turning myself into someone who can pass as a people person; if not a guy who bubbles with glee, then at least someone who can give the appearance of enjoying what he's doing.

And the surprising truth is, I am enjoying it. Weirdly, I'd never doubted I could teach the swing. Why I assumed I'd take so easily to pedagogy is a true mystery, but some things aren't meant to be explained. I've shown a real knack for identifying the particular obstacles each student has to overcome and figuring out how to help them do it. Strangely, I also seem to communicate some sort of quiet enthusiasm. None of which means I am looking forward to my last lesson of the day, which is with Matt from Dunbar. Given that Ross picked up his clubs and stormed off mid-session, I am surprised he even shows up. But Matt arrives on schedule, with a big smile and a warm handshake.

I've actually taken a couple of tune-up lessons from Matt, so this is another case of turnabout, and at first it isn't clear who is in charge. He begins by asking me to hit a few, which strikes me as reasonable enough for a pro. He also asks questions having to do with supination and pronation of the wrists, an arcane obsession of golf wonks and wankers dating all the way back to Ben Hogan. Perhaps there is an element of scrutiny in this, an attempt to see if the amateur knows what he is talking about, but I choose to regard it as genuine curiosity because Matt seems anything but skeptical about the swing. I would even call him enthusiastic, and this despite his own inability to make it work very well. We decide this is at least partly because he teaches and personally uses a David Leadbetter-style two-plane swing, whereas mine is predicated more on the Jim Hardy/Butch Harmon one-plane variety. Obviously, both of us have thought way more than a person really should about things like this. But if that makes Matt an unlikely convert, it doesn't stop him from admiring my demonstrations.

"Wow," he keeps saying as I stripe them out. "What are you playing to: Five? That's a joke. With your short game you're easily scratch now, probably better. You shot 70 on Sunday, right?"

"Yeah."

"The club championship is coming up. You're entering, right?"

"I suppose I should."

"Absolutely. Bill Jantz isn't around any more, and Charlie isn't what he once was. Hugh and Stan can both be had. I don't know who else there is. A bunch of twos and threes? I guess that guy Kevin Howell is getting pretty good. He's been playing a lot."

"He has?"

"Yeah, a lot."

The lesson is drawing to a close, which is good because I feel like my brain has suddenly turned into an echo chamber, in which everyone is "playing a lot." Or, if not everyone, then at least Syd and Kevin. And who could they be playing with? Is it possible that two people known to have carnal knowledge of each other are playing with themselves? That seems unlikely. In which case, why is Syd trying to make nice with me? Had my reaction to her and Kevin's evil and unnatural coupling been insufficiently emphatic?

As I turn into Dunbar my head is clouded with dark thoughts. Everybody is his or her own breed of dog, and some of us were simply born with the ball-chasing gene. I can't remember an occasion when my tail didn't involuntarily wag as I cruised down the lane.

But the mist doesn't lift when I get to the clubhouse and see Syd standing there, which is sad considering how good she looks. She's cut her hair a little shorter and maybe added a little orange to the mix, the better to set off an ensemble of the kind that only she can get away with: a rust-colored top matched with a vivid green skort, an item of clothing that sounds like a bad idea but on her never looks less than scintillating.

But time to suck it up. I've promised myself that if I am going to have to play the loser at love, I'll compensate by being the winner at golf. I'll pretend to be gracious early, she'll pretend to be gracious late. Appearances will be upheld, and there'll be no need for a security detail in a few weeks time when I return to win the club championship.

"Syd," I say. "So terribly good to see you. May I say you look brilliant."

If she is surprised to hear me speaking like a character out of one of P.G. Wodehouse's golf stories, she doesn't let on. Who knows, maybe she thinks I've spent the year casting for trout on an estate in Cornwall. In any event, she fairly leaps at me, insisting on giving me an enormous hug. "Jeff, I can't believe it's you. It's been so long."

I've always thought one of the reasons we got along so well is that she can tolerate my considerable reserve. She's certainly getting a full dose of it as I return the hug in a perfunctory manner and, for reasons unknown to me, reply, "Darling, it has been a while."

"We have a lot to talk about," she says. "But we're due on the tee."

"To the links!"

~ ~ ~ ~

What a change from Sunday: No-one else around, me playing the back tees, her on the front a full 95 yards ahead. I've always thought it must annoy women, especially women like Syd, that the usual 10 percent rule seems to have been waived for golf. In almost every other sport, men's elite performances are that much faster or farther. But a big-hitting pro crushes it 315 yards while the equivalent woman might do 275, and the differential is wider among ordinary players. Syd's handicap puts her in a rarefied group of women, whereas my similar one is of no particular note. Yet I expect to hit it 275 off the tee and she's happy with 210. From the front tees, at 425 yards, a monster 3-wood might get her to the green in two now and then, while from 520 I expect to reach more often than not, sometimes approaching with an iron.

So really, Dunbar and virtually every other course is set up in a way that is unfair to women—which, at the moment, is just fine with me. As usual our game will be match play, strictly for bragging rights; no money involved and definitely no sexual favors, as had regularly been the case in the old days, not that we discuss this. Neither of us needs extra incentive. We will be taking it seriously enough.

On the first hole my plan once again is to stay well away from the water. Alas, in the hour since I've left the range, I've tightened up a little, and I pull my drive, landing me in the rough. Up ahead Syd slyly puts away her driver and takes out a 3-wood, knocking it 190 yards straight down the fairway.

She hits another dead straight 3-wood to wedge range as I walk to where my ball should be, not that I can see it in Dunbar's notorious hay. But there it lies, deeply buried in the grass. Nothing to do but gouge it back out onto the fairway, with luck advancing it 60 or 70 yards, which is in fact what I manage to do, though not without inflicting some minor damage to my wrist.

I am now 160 yards to a front pin, a shot complicated by the likelihood that anything short will roll back off the green and along a short slope, leaving a tough up and down. For that reason I hit a smooth 7, which unfortunately bounces a good 25 feet past. Syd's pitching wedge does a little dance and settles about eight feet away. I two-putt, she sinks hers. One down.

As we walk to the second tee, Syd attempts to engage me in conversation of a serious nature.

"I can't get over this. God it's great to see you, Jeff. I missed you so much! How did this happen?"

You don't remember? Maybe something about Kevin Howell? "Stuff happens."

"Where did you disappear to? I wanted to talk to you so badly. I even hired a private detective."

Yeah, so you could slap me with a restraining order and then divorce me. "I have a little place."

"Look, we have to talk. I guess a lot of this is my fault. I'm so, so sorry."

Sure, apologize. What does it matter now. "Water under the bridge."

Our custom is to stop talking when the tee box is reached, and the moment I put my bag down Syd quiets. When I first joined the club the second hole was a tight old thing, with big shade trees hanging over. But that was before Sam and Syd got themselves voted onto the grounds committee and started agitating to have the course opened up. Way back when, father and daughter went on an Old Country golf holiday and came home convinced that Dunbar had been designed to be more of a heathland course, and the trees should be much sparser, leaving hummocks and scrub as the dominant upholstery. The membership didn't go for the fescue fairways they wanted to convert to, but did buy into a tree-removal program. No hole changed more than this one, which became something of a breather before the tough ones directly ahead. I fade a 3-wood through the car window, giving myself a 9-iron to the middle right pin. From 340 Syd pulls her own 3-wood into the first cut of rough, leaving about 160 to to the pin. With our balls separated by 40 yards, I walk up my side of the fairway, she hers, so I can't be sure what she hits, but in any case she misses it a shade and the ball stops rolling a few feet in front of the green. Now it's my turn to make a Pro-V dance, and that's what I do, sticking it 10 feet left of the pin.

With a fair bit of green to work with, Syd elects to bump and run a 9-iron, but it rolls eight feet past. She sunk one of that length a hole earlier and now she has the advantage of knowing her line, so I assume she'll plunk this one too, meaning mine has to drop. There is no discernible break, but the green is slightly canted and local knowledge would ordinarily have led me to take a half cup left. Instead, needing to be aggressive, I stroke it firmly toward the inside left edge, and that's where it stays, catching just enough of the hole. Back to even.

"You don't mind talking, do you? It would be so great if we could clear the air."

Yeah, so I don't kill Kevin the first time I see him with you. "Sure, no problem."

"OK, here goes: I know what you've been going through."

You think you know, but baby, you have no idea. "I've been OK."

"I've been going through it myself."

Sure you have. "Sorry to hear that."

"It's been the worst 12 months of my life."

What, a moment in your life that's been less than completely charmed? "Sorry to hear that."

After its so-so start, Dunbar gets it going on three, with a 460-yard par-4 that slopes down the valley to a green tucked inside a bend in Bratt Creek. The hole is as pretty as it is challenging, and in May, with the dogwoods still blooming, it's enough to make a person cry, which is what I secretly want to do.

Filigreed fairway bunkers left and right add to the hole's esthetic appeal, but don't really come into play with modern clubs and balls, so it's bombs away. With no need to steer my driver, I pound out that beautiful thing, a towering draw, which provokes an appreciative sigh from Syd and figures to leave me a short-iron to the pin. From 370 Syd also makes a decent swing but is still 10 yards behind me.

On her approach Syd is looking at about 170 yards, maybe a 3-iron or fairway-wood, which is not what you want to be hitting downhill to a green with big trouble right and long. Another glaring case of gender bias, since I will be floating in an 8-iron. But cancel the human rights tribunal: Her ball lands just in front of the green and pops up smartly, rolling to 20 feet. Forced to take an aggressive line, I block mine a touch right, and watch it bounce sideways off the fringe, probably into the creek.

At worst, Syd is going to two-putt for par, so finding myself still alive on the edge of the stream is only a minor relief. But miraculously I manage to get my 60-degree wedge cleanly on the ball, which flops up to five feet. I concede Syd's two-footer, then sink my own. Still even.

"Did you know I had to take a leave of absence from work?"

"Really, you did? That must have been tough on you."

"Thank god for golf."

On that we can agree. "No kidding."

"I kept hoping I'd see you here."

Maybe you shouldn't have humiliated me with a restraining order then. "It wasn't to be."

The sigh of relief after three is replaced by a sigh of resignation when you reach the hilltop tee box and see what's in store. At 430 yards the fourth isn't huge but it plays right down the creek, which in fact loops into it about halfway along. I have two options: carry the bend at 255 or hit a 3-iron to no more than 225, leaving a long iron or even fairway wood to a mercifully generous landing area and green. Were I down I might pull out the driver, but Syd figures to have a tough par so I decide to go with the iron, which could not be more exquisitely struck.

Syd's only reasonable option is to take the long way, which is patently unfair, and will turn the hole into a probable three-shooter for her.

But in 30 years she has played the hole maybe 4,000 times and isn't going to whine about it now. She hits a soaring drive that probably would have cleared the water had she decided to go for it, but in any case leaves her no more than 175 from the pin. This is immaterial to me, however. My simple task is to strike another iron with exquisite perfection, landing my ball on or just before the green and letting it bounce up to the pin. And that is what I do. Syd's 5-wood follows, but a little too eagerly, bounding across the green into the rough at back left.

There she finds a decent lie in an area of short grass, which is fortunate for her because I am only about 15 feet from the pin. Syd never used to be a great chipper, so I am stunned when she plays a low spinner, an advanced shot that I practice all the time but might not have the courage to use in a competitive situation. It checks up a few feet from the hole and stops no more than three feet behind. I don't know if I misread my putt or pull it a shade, but it lips out left. Syd sinks hers. Still even.

"I was clinically depressed. I actually thought about suicide."

Wouldn't that have been sad for poor Kevin. "I'm so sorry."

"I never wanted a restraining order. I didn't want to divorce you."

You didn't? "Crazy world."

"Everything would have been fine. We could have gotten over it if you hadn't started poisoning the garden."

Maybe you would have gotten over it. "You think I'd do a thing like that?"

The fifth at Dunbar is a nasty par-3 running alongside the creek. It's only 175 yards, but there's water left and the valley wall to the right is covered in a clumpy grass that generally holds the ball and is hard to play out of, so there's nothing to do but hit it straight. Having just blocked a shot, I aim my 6-iron at the centre of the green rather than the safer right side, tugging it a little but holding the back left fringe about 25 feet from the pin. From 140 Syd also chooses 6-iron and makes much the same shot, although her putt stays inside of mine.

A three-putt is always a possibility on the steeply sloping green, but I am reasonably content to run it four feet past. I concede Syd's gimme and study my knee knocker, with its right to left break. My stroke is perfect and the ball would have dropped but it pulls up in the last foot and stops an inch short. Incredibly, I have made the simple mental mistake of forgetting that my putt is also slightly uphill. Down one.

"I know it was you. The Andersons saw you. They have it on video."

Oh. "Oh."

"I was scared. You were acting so weird."

Wow, busted. "I guess that might have seemed a little strange."

"A little strange? What would it have been next? My cat?"

Your cat! That was our cat. "Lucca? Oh, come on!"

Suddenly down one I have to revise my strategy for six, another beaut. Just 320 yards long and slightly downhill, it's almost reachable. Were I even or ahead, I'd play an iron and take my routine par, but the way she's playing, Syd is going to do no worse than that, so I decide to pull out the driver. The trouble is mostly on the left, so I park the Olds at 270 and set up a shade open. I can't see where the ball ends up, but I know I've sailed it right over the Cutlass's hideous formal roof, so there's no way it is going to be more than 10 yards short. Syd hits a 5-wood to 80 yards, and from there we can see that my ball has almost rolled on. She lands her pitching wedge two feet from the pin, but it doesn't bite and she is left with a 15-footer. I am only 30 feet from the pin but not quite on the fringe, so I have to decide whether to putt or chip. Figuring a birdie will take it and certain I can chip to two or three feet, I choose my pitching wedge but chunk it a shade, leaving myself five feet short. Syd misses, I make. Even.

"Look, what was I supposed to do? You'd blown up a Porsche, pissed all over someone's bed and laptop, vandalized a lawn, and now you were sneaking into the garden and pouring herbicide on the rhododendrons."

But I wasn't in the hot tub with Kevin Howell. "I never said you did the wrong thing."

"Even that I might have overlooked if you hadn't been wearing a camouflage suit."

I agree completely. The suit was egregious. "What can I say?"

"If only you'd say something. I'm doing all the talking. I thought everything was supposed to be different."

What six gives, seven takes away. A 450-yard dogleg left, it requires a drive of 240 just to make the corner. In the old days, if the wind was against me, I played it as a three-shotter. Not today, though. I park the Olds in the middle of the fairway and make that smooth, smooth swing, but somehow hit the ball a little off the heel, which results in a weak fade. This is ominous, because for once Dunbar has a little something for the ladies, specifically a front tee 120 yards closer to the hole. Syd draws it around the corner perfectly and will be no more than 130 from the pin.

To the left of the green are trees, bunkers and nasty rough, to the right there's a little ravine. It doesn't really come into play except for slicers, but both fairway and green slope toward it, making it necessary to cheat left with the four-iron I am going to have to play. Back when I was hooking, I'd posted some high scores here. Nothing to do but go for it, though, as Syd figures to be giving herself a birdie chance.

What a great swing I make. Unfortunately, my ball stays dead straight instead of fading a touch as my lie had led me to expect. Syd calmly hits a seven-iron that ends about 20 feet back right of the pin.

From the greenside bunker I am going to have to get it up and down, a strength of my game and something I expect to accomplish an impressive two-thirds of the time. But in the past 11 months I've made 10,000 shots out of Bill's practice bunker compared to zero out of Dunbar's real ones, and I've forgotten that the sand at the course is a little looser. The ball flies two or three feet by the spot I'd chosen for it to land and then fails to check on the slight downslope, rolling a good eight feet past. If there's a positive, it's that Syd will give me the line with her 20-footer. Stationing myself out of her field of vision but close enough that I can study the last 10 feet of her roll, I watch as she assesses the putt then steps up and made a firm, fluid stroke, no doubt having chanted her mantra: "Left shoulder up, ball in the cup."

Well, it doesn't go in the cup, but it does lip out for yet another conceded par, which means I must make. Once again there is no discernible break to the putt, and Syd's stayed dead straight as far as I could tell. Yet, I remember this green having a slight back-to-front slope, so I decide to take enough of the hole that the ball will drop if it stays straight but also if it curls an inch or so. Sure enough, it bends ever so slightly toward the centre of the cup—but then veers visibly back on line, somehow failing to drop as it curves along the right side of the cup. I look at the green and spot an unrepaired gouge at the very spot where my ball changed direction. What an idiotic amateur mistake. Down one.

"Not your fault," Syd says, reading my mind. "Rub of the green. It's a flagstick dent. You couldn't have repaired it anyway."

Silence.

"Rule 16-1c."

Silence

"Jeff, are you there? Anybody home?"

Silence.

"I give up."

Thank god for my new routine. At a time like this, when conscious thought is beyond me, I can still perform my little rituals, step up to the ball and make a good swing, which is all a person has to do on eight, a pretty but straightforward par-3 that plays to an imposing 220 yards. Thwack. A slight draw brings my 3-iron back to the middle of the green, only a few feet short, leaving me a birdie try. From 150 the other person in my group bounces it right by the pin but to the back of the green, a good 25 feet past.

I am assaying my putt from the front when something Syd is up to catches my eye. She and I are in agreement about many things having to do with the game of golf, including the role of plumb bobbing, which is more likely to be done poorly than well, and thus should be avoided. Yet, there she is in the classic crouching position, her putter hanging from her right hand directly in front of her dominant right eye. And that's when I notice something else that seems odd. The bright green item of fashionable women's golfing apparel that I had taken to be a skort isn't that at all. It's a skirt. Moreover, true to historic form, Syd has neglected to wear standard underpinnings. I glance up at her eyes and see that she isn't looking at her ball but rather at me. Suddenly my mouth starts moving, even before it receives a signal from my brain. "Syd," it somehow says. "You've shaved."

"A miracle—he speaks," she says, before taking her stance and putting to within a foot for another concession.

And it is a miracle. Within seconds the fog completely clears and I can think like a regular human being—a heterosexual, male human, to be sure. Sinking my seven-footer is the first priority, of course, one that I promptly achieve. "Syd," I say as we walk off the green, once again even. "Thank you so much. I needed that."

"Always a pleasure. Now, can we talk?"

And we do—small talk, but talk nevertheless—all the way up the difficult 560-yard ninth, which we both reach without mishap in three. I've already putted to three feet when Syd starts to size up her 30-footer. She's chosen her line and is ready to take her stance when I say, "Are you completely sure of that putt?" Under any other other circumstances, this would be regarded as chauvinism or gamesmanship, a deplorable breach in either case, but under these Syd takes it in the spirit intended.

"Actually, no," she says. "I think I better plumb bob it."

And that's what she does, bless her. There is nothing to do but applaud when the subtle double breaker finds the cup for a birdie. Syd wins, one up.

CHAPTER 3
TILTING

SYDNEY, MAY 10, 2007

Shameful. The things a woman will do. Yesterday, for example—a new low.

What's that they say about desperate times? Let's hope I'm wrong, but the boomtown stuff seems to be dwindling away, and the firm has to get something big on the books. So hey, says the usually steadfast Sydney, let's abandon our principles! Last year and the year before that and, well, forever, we were all about the Onward of Architecture. Yes, that's our ever so high-brow motto, a sly if admittedly pretentious reference to the British sculptor Anthony Caro and his "Onward of Art."

We were the firm that wouldn't cave in to crass market realities. We'd tailor and refine. We'd toss a month of work in the garbage if it wasn't going where it needed to go. But we wouldn't pander, we wouldn't lay on the glitz. No trips into decorator land for us.

But suddenly there's a contract on the line because the clients think our design is too "European," what with it being such a shimmering, fluid expression of uncanny functionality and eternal beauty. So what do I say? "That's a very perceptive critique. Perhaps the external poetics lack the emphasis implied by the underlying structure."

Who knows what I was talking about? Who knows what poetry is in the context of architecture? Who knows what poetics are, period? Well, apparently the clients do, because their faces brightened right up. So I leaned over the table and promised we'd have a revised proposal for Tuesday.

I have no idea how to improve something that was already perfect. That's why I'm here at the office with partner Bob on a Saturday morning. He's performing some last-minute magic on temporary facilities that we all agree have to be too too when the Gay Games arrive to grace our town after only 57 more sleeps. I'm here giving some mortgage company's new headquarters what can only be described as bigger tits.

And, well, speaking of artificial enhancements, how weird is that this morning I'd run into Carrie? She's looking really good, too. Back here from Denver, but hasn't even said hi to Kevin. Hunting for a sales job, but not in real estate. Too many bad vibes, she says.

We agreed to get together some evening. Memo to self: don't drink too much. Mom's developed an odd puritan streak lately, but I have to admit she isn't far off about the perils of alcohol. Prevents heart disease but causes naked swan dives into empty swimming pools. Personal experience, no doubt.

Are we doomed to be our parents? One might think so—until one remembered Jeff and his mom. That poor kid. How could you not want to look after someone who's been through what he has? It's hilarious the way he keeps everything to himself, revealing only a little at a time, never telling the whole truth. Shutting it all in, then blowing it all out. And then you begin to understand. Conceived and raised as a science project!

He didn't tell me, of course. I still wouldn't know if it weren't for Masa—the self-described control group. Midori trained as a plant geneticist, unusual for a woman in the 1960s, let alone someone in Japan, but apparently she was brilliant, as hard as it is to comprehend. Those must have been exciting times: the beginning of the Green Revolution, Japan coming into its own like that. Not quickly enough for Midori, though. In Tokyo she hooked up with a pro ball player but never married him, even after getting pregnant with Masa. No doubt there were limits to what a single mom could get away with, even Midori, which may have been why she decided to come here for her doctorate. Masa isn't sure when the grand plan began to take shape but he thinks the interest in human genetics wasn't really sparked until after her arrival. In Japan she would have had limited experience with anyone who wasn't Japanese, and suddenly she was surrounded by people from all over the world. Her doctoral research focused on hybrids, and she would have known that heterosis is as potent with pets and livestock as with rice and corn. To her it must have seemed that white folks and Japanese were at least as distinct as Holsteins and Herefords. Could hybrid vigor be exploited to create superior humans?

That was the bee in her bonnet, and when Midori's brain is buzzing, take cover. Still, it was the late 1960s, and even if Hitler and the KKK hadn't tainted things so thoroughly, there wasn't going to be any money for a research project focusing on the breeding of turbo-charged, mixed-race humans. So Midori decided to do it on the cheap. Obviously, she would have recognized the limitations. The role of environment, the natural variation in offspring, the exceptionally small sample size. She knew she would be creating anecdote, not data, but the bees were buzzing, so she set out to design as sound an experiment as she could.

It's all there in her careful notes. She began by establishing a baseline, subjecting Masa to a battery of physical, psychological and developmental tests at age two, then repeating them annually with both boys for the next 14 years, stopping only after they refused to play along.

Then there was the matter of finding an appropriate father for the second subject, one as similar as possible to Masa's dad. So she got hold of his baseball stats back in Japan: batting average, on-base average, slugging percentage, stolen bases, fielding percentage, assists—even then the game was uniquely proficient at painting a digital picture of a person's physical attributes. Because she'd gone out with Father No. 1 for a few weeks, Midori also felt comfortable filling in a few additional details, including IQ, which she estimated at 130—probably about right as he went on to become an executive at Sony after his playing days.

She knew where to look when it came to initiating production of the B sample, of course: the bar favored by players on the Triple-A team. Before she stepped inside the padded-vinyl door, she subjected every player's stats to an equally careful analysis, looking for exactly the kind of speedy, line-drive hitter that had sired Masa.

She turned up two matches, apparently, but one stood out as ideal: another shortstop, this one on the fast track to the major leagues, where he would subsequently enjoy a respectable career before moving on to become a corporate executive, much like Masa's dad. Unfortunately, this hot prospect was a devout Mormon, and when Midori showed up at the Red Lion, he was nowhere to be found. She checked her notes, and quickly identified her backup, the team's second baseman, a 22-year-old rookie who had no idea he was about to contribute his body to science.

I can imagine the scene. Just a few months out of Japan and with only a basic command of English, Midori probably hadn't recognized Hector Ramon as anything other than an American name. She would have asked someone a question like: "Which player Mr. Ramon?" A finger would have been pointed. Then, maybe some brief confusion, a moment of thought as she reviewed the outline of her study. Or maybe it didn't matter that the young

Nicaraguan she was directed to was of primarily African descent. Negro, Caucasian: as long as the father wasn't Asian, her offspring would be taller, stronger and smarter if the heterosis thesis proved out. Either way, science would be served.

The young ball player's English would have been even worse than hers, but presumably that did not prevent Midori from ascertaining to her satisfaction that he was of appropriate intelligence. In any case, there was only one step remaining. Did she form a circle with her left thumb and forefinger and repeatedly insert her right forefinger while gesturing toward the door? Well, it's rarely difficult for a reasonably appealing and definitely exotic woman to convince a young athlete to take her back to his room for a thankfully undescribed sex act. Nine months later Jeff was born and the experiment entered Phase 2.

Incredibly enough, the boys find Midori's notes on their upbringing to be even more painful than those pertaining to the breeding program that produced them. The only source of relief is knowing that the article detailing their progress was rejected for publication by several academic journals.

Put simply, Midori came to the conclusion that heterosis in mixed-race humans remained a likely proposition but could not be proven, based on her observation of two half-brothers: "a mixed-race Asian/Negro specimen and an Asian control subject." Over the course of some 30 pages, she detailed the developmental progress of each: Masa racing along in the top decile of his cohort group; Jeff limping along a decile or two behind. Her conclusion: "By almost all measures, the mixed-race Negro/Asian specimen performs at a lower level than either the half-brother control subject or the Negro/Asian's direct genetic antecedents, providing no support for the heterosis hypothesis."

Well, you can imagine how Jeff came to feel about all of this, especially as he can be a little touchy. The more I came to know him, the more I recognized how darkly loomed the spectre of

Dr. Jekyll and Ms. Hyde. None of which was going to make an upcoming weekend anything less than an awkward time.

We were having a drink and something to eat in the clubhouse when my phone buzzed. I shouldn't have had it on, but I had to talk to partner Bob about the headquarters and its sudden need for augmentation. Who knows what Jeff was thinking, considering what had transpired on those greens. Sex with the ex has its place, I believe, but we weren't headed to bed, even if on ethical grounds I was going to have a hard time demurring.

"Hello,"

"Sydney, is that you?"

"Midori?" (Worried glance toward Jeff. Distressed look back.)

"Sydney, you have to help me find Hiroshi."

"Midori, how are you? Is everything OK?"

"I'm fine. You have to get Hiroshi." (Frantic head shaking. Hands involuntarily raised into the "don't hit me" position.)

"We were divorced last year. There was a restraining order. You know all that."

"Sydney, he'll talk to you. Tell him I'm coming to see him." (Convincing imitation, also spontaneous, of Munch's "The Scream.")

"Midori, we're divorced. Maybe Masa…"

"Tell him to call me." (Pushing back chair.)

Tell him it has to do with his father." (Slight hesitation. Fight or flight response fading?)

"Really?"

"He's coming to see him. Soon. It's very important that I talk to Hiroshi."

"OK. No promises. Good-bye."

"Jeff, where did you go? Jeff!"

~ ~ ~ ~

God, that was terrible. I hope no-one else saw. Syd standing in the middle of the road like that with her skirt lifted up to her waist. Does she think her vagina has magic powers?

Still, you have to appreciate the thought. She really is a sport. It's a tragedy the way things are between us. Mom and I—that's a different story. But I will call her. Really, I will.

I wonder if she's been in touch with old Ramon all these years? Quite the pair they'd make. Did make, I guess. The horror.

It's odd that he was able to track her down if what she's always said is true. No contact since conception and a subsequent note advising him of my existence, she swears. Fortunately, she wouldn't be aware of my own near-dad experience—yet another Jeff Jones communication triumph, this one dating back to 1990. I was taking a year off to rethink school, having finally recognized that cultural studies wouldn't get me anywhere that didn't involve the frequent asking of that most existential of questions: For here or to go?

The ways she screwed me up. I could have made my future life easier by studying something useful, like basket weaving, but no, I pursue a degree in cultural studies, a social science intent on refuting her damned science, a discipline so far up its ass, it can see sociology's heels. The crap we studied. Then again, one of the arrows in its tiny quill is the concept of agency, which means, I dunno, I guess that I possessed the capacity to make decisions. As such I decided to journey to Nicaragua, which was in the midst of epochal elections following 10 years of Sandinista rule. My goals were to A) assist, if I could, the Sandinistas in their election bid, and B) find my father, with luck a Sandinista himself.

It was B) that excited me most. Perhaps I simply lacked immunity to standard human emotions, but probably I'd also been influenced by Masa's experience. After a poignant reunion, his father had warmly welcomed him into the big, happy extended family, convincing him to move to Japan and setting him up in what had turned out be a rewarding career. Among other benefits, this allowed Masa to live an entire hemisphere away from mom without ever pointedly rejecting her.

Not that our situations are comparable. Masa's dad was aware of his bastard child's existence and even maintained contact with Mom. Meanwhile, she and Ramon met only once, so she said, long enough for an informal job interview and brief collaboration on the science fair project. All I knew of my sire were his career stats in America: a few weeks at Single-A, then a jump to the Triple-A team, the kind of rapid progression that usually signals an impending major-league career. He finished the season batting .304, with 11 homers, eight triples, 37 doubles and 56 stolen bases. Then he opened 1969 with an eye-popping .388 average and 18 steals in 26 games, before simply disappearing. A microfiche search of newspaper records shed no additional light on his sudden departure, but I had my suspicions about what happened: Mom showed up at BP one day early in the season with babe in arms and beckoned him over. Perhaps there was talk of a financial arrangement, as was the case with Masa's dad; perhaps even an attempt on her part to resume the "relationship." Probably, he took one look into her eyes and knew his life would be hell as long as he remained in the same half of the same nation, a recognition I know all too well. In any case he suddenly decided that a career mucking around in central America didn't look so bad and stole back home to Nicaragua.

I expected that, in a country of less than five million people, it wouldn't be hard to find a man who might have been one of the best native-son players ever—who might even still be playing. When I arrived there I could see how naive I'd been. After a devastating earthquake and decades of civil war, the country was in a shambles. I quickly fell in with the young aid workers and fellow cultural studies dropouts who were making Managua one of the globe's most happening cities that year, and tried to lend a hand to the Sandinista cause, though in truth my main contribution was to increase the country's dismal GDP with my heroic beer consumption. I was still formulating a plan for how I'd track down Hector Ramon when I brought up his name at a long, crowded table in a typically crappy bar.

Conversation hushed. "You mean *the* Hector Ramon?"

"I don't know. All I know is he's a second baseman who played a couple of years on my hometown minor-league team."

"Baseball player? That would be Hector Ramon."

"Really? He's still playing?"

Big laugh. "No, he's still killing peasants and shipping coke to Oliver North. He's a major-league contra."

"Oh. Apparently he could sure turn a double play."

Detection averted, coolness preserved. Who was that being so quick on his feet? The conversation shifted back to talk of that new music coming out of Seattle and which of REM or U2 had sold out their college radio cred most thoroughly.

But at least I had something to go on, even if it wasn't what I'd hoped for, so I embarked on some research into Hector Ramon. Nothing genuinely enterprising like actually talking to anyone, but I did make it to the library at UNAN, the university there, where I was able to look in newspaper archives. Sure enough, Ramon arrived back in the country in 1970. The country's own pro league had folded a couple of years earlier, but he played on what seems to have been a semi-pro tournament team as well as leagues elsewhere in Latin America. Wherever he went, he proved to be a star, a perennial MVP who had the local sports writers wondering why he didn't play in the States when it was so plainly obvious he could have.

Gradually Ramon moved off the sports pages and into the front section. As a baseball star, he made for a high-profile opponent to Daniel Ortega's Sandinistas, and during the campaign he was given to making appearances in aid of Violeta Chamorro, the election victor and Ortega's successor. I went to a rally and, sure enough, there he was. A fit-looking man standing 5' 10", exactly as his stats said. Except for the relative darkness of his skin and complete absence of slanty eyes, he also looked pretty much like me, which was equally predictable but still shocked me to the shuddering core. The next day I cut out of Nicaragua to shepherd my last few hundred dollars hanging out by the beach in Costa Rica, a country that seemed safer and easier to sleep in.

And now we are going to be reunited. That is, assuming I possess the strength of will and tolerance for abuse to pick up the phone and call Mom.

"Hello."

"Hi, Mom."

"Hiroshi! My son! Alive!"

"It's been awhile, I guess."

"Eight months!"

"Well, how have you been?"

"Heartsick. My own son won't talk to me."

"I guess I somehow expected that my mom wouldn't convince my wife to divorce me."

"I was concerned for her safety. Your strange behavior. The Latin blood. It was my fault, so I dealt with it. I was taking responsibility."

"Jesus. Never mind. What's this about my dad?"

"Very strange. He contacted me. No idea how."

"You haven't secretly been getting money from him all these years like you were from Masa's dad?"

"No! I had no contact. I told you that. Just the note after you were born. I don't understand at all. Then yesterday the phone rang. His English is a lot better, I can tell you. Very good. But it's you he wants to see, except he didn't know how to contact you. He didn't know your name. Maybe changing it from Hiroshi Nakamura to Jeff Jones wasn't such a good idea?"

"But why? Did he say anything else?"

"No. Just that he'll be arriving in eight weeks. Exciting, right?"

"Right."

I hang up with two thoughts. Yes, this is exciting. And now my mother knows my phone number.

～ ～ ～ ～

SYDNEY

I've asked myself many times what I saw in him. Almost as many times as others have asked it of me.

I don't know that the initial attraction had much to do with thinking he was a black guy. First, he really did have some interesting things to say about urban planning. OK, I know that sounds unlikely, but let's not forget I'm an architect and there is some overlap. Oh sure, he was naive and idealistic in the way that students usually are—a big fan of so-called New Urbanism, for example. He thought that most of the world's problems would be solved if everyone lived in walkable mixed-use neighbourhoods and had a front porch to wave at the neighbours from. Never mind that most of the proponents are nostalgists who want us to live in houses that look like they date from 1910. Enemies of architecture, that's what they are. A share of the blame will be on their shoulders when people eventually recognize the tragedy of having such an enormous housing boom and so little of value to show for it.

But Jeff, well, he listened to what I had to say and seemed to get that privileging some romantic idea of street appeal over function and livability is evil. And OK, he did look pretty fit, and I suppose I was a little curious. When we got to bed, he seemed to feel it necessary to explain that he was half-Japanese. After that we always called it Mr. In Between.

He moved in with me after the second date, if that's the right word for getting hammered, falling into bed and trying to screw. Crazy, I know, but it was just so easy. I was curious how mom and dad would react when I brought him home for the first time. Everyone looks at our family and sees a model of tolerance and liberal values, but they don't understand. Dad's a farm boy who studied engineering; Mom may have done a little too much acid. Just when you least expect, he's early Clint Eastwood and she's late Shirley Maclaine.

Jeff was nervous, of course. He's always secretly nervous. An intelligent but essentially unperceptive guy who, conversely, is constantly watching himself and can see how unperceptive he is? Yeah, a person like that might be a bit nervous. And of course there's the knowledge that he's the one who gets lynched the day we stumble through the space-time continuum and end up in 1960s-era Alabama. But he was really on edge that day.

"They'll know we're having sex, won't they?"

"I'm 26. You're not the first boy I've brought home."

"But all of the others were white."

"You think that's a parent's main concern? Roger was out on parole. Matt was a skinhead. Todd played in a punk band long after it was fashionable. Justin was a Baha'i. Peter was 32. Trevor was visibly erect."

"You told me I was your first."

"I said you were my first urban planning student. Well, my first urban planning graduate student. My first male urban planning graduate student. OK, and this is the truth, I've never had sex with anyone—man, woman or transgendered—writing his, her or its urban planning thesis on development conflicts in established neighborhoods."

Ba-da-boom. He laughed at the little routine, a good sign as all I'd usually get was a half smile that could be read as either wry or pained. If he was really, really happy, he might break out whistling, but chuckles, those were rare.

And not to worry about the meet-the-parents thing, as it turned out, at least not from Jeff's end. Honestly, I think Mom had reverted to her old pothead ways. Otherwise, I doubt she would have been so eager to take us back to her studio and show Jeff her paintings, among them a selection from my art modeling interlude. "So now you know, Jeff," I said. "The carpet matches the drapes."

Mom *must* have been stoned. Otherwise she would have caught the note in my voice; recognized that perhaps Jeff wasn't familiar with my bush. But, no. "I work with photographs as well," she said, moving to get one of the big portfolios where she kept her prints.

Which stage of her career would we get? Tantalizing the new boyfriend with more nudes of me would be creepy, but even worse would be her still lifes of flowers, mollusks and other vulva lookalikes. They're the artistic equivalent of architectural post-modernism as executed by an acolyte of the Memphis Group. If an artist's career can be measured by the weakest link in the chain, well, say no more.

But Mom had a surprise: some new work, and I have to say it looked terrific. Big color pictures of banal exurban scenes—the kinds of places where crappy new subdivisions brush up against abandoned farms and hubcap emporia.

In retrospect I suppose she borrowed a little too heavily from the work of artists like Jeff Wall and Andreas Gursky, but this was 1996, and they weren't exactly household names back then, at least not to people who'd let their subscriptions to *Artforum* lapse. Mom explained to us how the pictures had come about. "I picked up an old 8 x 10 format camera," she said. "I've always liked to work with a larger format, you know, but the really big cameras are amazing."

She wasn't wrong about that. Jeff was knocked out, of course. He was not a sophisticated appreciator of art, and there was a certain showiness to the pictures. I didn't realize till later that one of the attributes of large-format cameras is the immense depth of field they're capable of, which keeps distant objects in much sharper focus than the human eye is accustomed to. The effect of seeing all that detail can be mesmerizing, and Mom had cleverly used some sort of luminous metallic paper, which heightened the effect. Being young and male, Jeff would have dug the inherent irony in those scenes. But beyond all that, I think it was the subject matter that appealed to him. Not people, not the landscape—the way people fuck up the landscape. Perfect for a misanthropic social scientist. More charitably, to an idealistic young planner-to-be, here was proof positive that there was work to be done.

I liked the work as well, and I couldn't believe how relieved I felt. A big camera like that isn't made for shooting people, so perhaps the choice of subject matter was more practical than anything else. Still, I examined the pictures for sexual themes, deliberate or subconscious, and if they were there they escaped me. I've never quite figured out whether mom was the original post-feminist riot grrrl or a mere pre-feminist libertine, but either way the relentless focus on sexuality was getting to be a little much. Sure, the absence of repression can only be regarded as healthy, but she was getting dangerously close to becoming, if I can be forgiven for even thinking this, *Playboy*'s udderly insatiable granny.

When we'd arrived on that Sunday afternoon, Dad wasn't at the house but golfing. He walked the few blocks to the club pretty much every day he was in town and not off on one of his marketing expeditions. He'd have been well into his 50s then, and needed the constant practice to stay scratch and beat the young bucks who outdrove him by 20 yards.

I've always been a Daddy's girl, I guess. As a teenager I assumed my irritation with Mom would dissipate as I grew older, as the books on child development I was given to reading assured would be the case. But in fact, we never quite bonded, and I think the damn sex thing was part of it. I wouldn't call Dad a prude, but he always understood that children don't want to know anything about their parent's sexuality, or even their anatomy. So while mom routinely cruised naked out by the pool, Dad's dress code always involved clothes. And of course, there wasn't a library of his self-published erotica in the house, as was the case with mom.

Still, I have to give both mom and dad a lot of credit for being so decent with my boyfriends. In retrospect I guess the problem with being a precocious little girl who learns to read at four and at 12 can hold forth on geopolitics and esthetics is that, way too soon, you think you're ready to sleep your way through the rowing team or, in my case, the docket court. What would I do if my little girl brought home a cokehead who'd recently lost his job as a late-night deejay at the AOR station? At the very least there'd be a discussion about the legal concept of statutory rape, which, come to think of it, probably happened, with Dad in full make-my-day mode.

After most of those guys, Jeff would have come across as a complete gentleman. No wonder they were so nice to him, drawing him out, trying so hard to care about urban planning. Jeff responded too, talking at some length about New Urbanism, and how great the house was, and how it might be even better if they renovated to put a veranda in front. I wasn't in agreement, of course, but it was nice to have such a spirited discussion. After dinner I realized the only person who hadn't had his moment was Dad, and it would be terrible not to expose a new boyfriend to someone whose work is always so interesting.

"So Dad," I said. "What contraption from days of yore have you been repurposing for our ever-changing world?"

"Nothing much at the moment. Still riding that gas station thing. Just back from a quick trip to Kazakhstan. Who'd have thought five years ago that they'd be ready for self-serve?"

Modest as always. "Nothing percolating in that lab of yours? We checked out Mom's studio"—sidelong glance—"Let's see your den of iniquity."

"Yes, dear. The kids will want to see your lab." Mom jumped in with a smile, no doubt having missed my pointed remark.

"Nothing to see just now. I'll fire up the Bunsen burners next time."

But Mom was already leading the way.

"Wow," said Jeff, a typical reaction when people see Dad's lab for the first time. Walking through the door is like stepping from one of James Bond's more restrained pads into M's lab. Back in 1970, when they bought the house, Dad spared no expense outfitting the room as his world headquarters, but before long he was spending most of his time on the road or on the course, and a lot of the equipment had hardly ever been used.

"There really is a Bunsen burner," said Jeff, who was in quite the conversational mood.

"What's this, Dad?" I said, pointing at something that was probably his next patent office project.

"Just a prototype. Nothing important," he said.

"Now dear," said Mom—sidelong glance of her own—"tell the kids what you're working on."

"Well," he said. "It's a marital aid. Anyone for a scotch?"

"Really, Dad?" I looked for some vaguely appropriate parts, but it was like nothing I'd ever seen.

Dad wasn't talking. "It's for the … *husband*," Mom said with a smile.

"Really?"

"Dear, tell them where the idea came from."

"Well, uh, there was a lot of innovation associated with the shoe-shine business during World War II."

"Dad, are you changing the subject?"

"No. There was a terrible labor shortage during the war, as you probably know, and men still thought they had to have shiny shoes, so a lot of thinking went into how machines could do the job."

The light bulb goes on. "You've adapted shoe-shine technology to the penis?" I said this very slowly.

"Here's an interesting statistic. In the past decade, sales of aids for women have exploded. For the prime 19-49 demographic we're now approaching 60 percent market, uh, penetration."

Awed silence.

"Yet there's no similar trend for men. Why is that? You could argue that men have less need for a helping hand, or that the devices lack utility, but it's equally true that women have benefited from tremendous investment into research and development."

"More technologically advanced vibrators?"

"It's hardly a secret," Dad smiled at me. His salesman instincts were taking over, which was unfortunate.

"There's also a demographic case," he said. "Two generations ago the average age of marriage for men was 24. Today that doesn't occur till 30. Some of those men are living with women, but many are on their own, so what are they doing?"

God help me, caught up by his salesman patter, with my right hand I made the jerk-off motion.

"Exactly!" he said. "But what if there were a marital aid that enhanced the experience, that added a whole new dimension? So I've also adapted technology from the gaming industry." Sure enough, there was a joystick hooked up to the device. "The gentleman can program it as he sees fit, explore several different pre-sets or revert to manual mode and manipulate it using the—I believe it's called a joystick." He smiled. "Appropriate, don't you think?"

By then I had vowed not to fall into any more of his rhetorical traps, nor in fact to utter anything at all. Dad had also said enough, and the four of us stood looking at the contraption for as long as we could bear, then filed out of the room in silence.

~ ~ ~ ~

JEFF, MAY 13

The transition to a more normal kind of life is happening much faster than I could have imagined. I realize this when I pick up the phone to call mom and hear the message-waiting beep, the first time this has occurred in almost a year. After hanging up, I punch *98—memory like a steel trap!—and discover that not one but two people have called, all in the space of five hours.

The first message is from Jenny. On that first evening we discussed my shyness and recent tendency to go months without talking to others of the species and agreed that if we were ever going to see one another again—and we both hoped we would—it would be because she took the initiative. "Hey Jeff, How about Monday? You can give me another lesson and then we'll go somewhere. Not sure where yet, but my treat this time. Does half-past six work? Call me. Bye for now."

Isn't that nice? And what an object of female lust I am getting to be. Admittedly there were extenuating circumstances, but on my last date a very attractive woman exposed her genitalia on three occasions; now another is phoning with plans to ply me with drinks.

The second message is from Bill. "Hey Jeff, we have to get you a cell phone. Did you catch the new *Golf Digest*? See you tomorrow morning."

I don't even realize I am whistling when I stop in at the little store across the street from the complex, but so I am assured by the young clerk I've been nodding to for the past several months.

"Hey, dig the Nirvana tune. I had you more as the Hootie and the Blowfish type."

I take this as one-third grudging compliment, two thirds sly put-down. That's the trouble with golf headwear. Until you work up the courage to switch to a hat—something in the style of Sam Snead, not Greg Norman or Briny Baird, please—you're stuck in a cap, and, if I may be allowed a cultural studies moment, caps are potent signifiers. As fashion accessories, flat caps and paperboys seem to work or not work on a more or less random basis, but let's agree they imply a certain confidence and perhaps something of a hipster inclination. A trucker's cap knocks 20 points off your perceived IQ, it's said, while a baseball cap seems to have bimodal characteristics. Worn with Levis and a leather jacket, you're a middle-aged Rotisserie Leaguer, inevitably 40 pounds overweight; with a hoodie, big pants and a flat brim, a wannabe gangbanger wishing you were packing heat. But a golf cap has one straightforward message: "Damn right I'm an affluent guy with a house in the suburbs, and I didn't get that way by being edgily creative."

"Yeah, Hootie rocks," I reply, staring down at the *Golf Digest* and its monthly promise to knock several strokes off my game. "But I think he's better as a solo act."

Back in the Neon I leaf through the magazine, anxious to get to the cover story—the stroke-saving, handicap-busting, game-changing new wrinkle of the month.

Turn page, turn page, hmmm, now there's a shiny new driver, and—what's this? *Holy fucking shit! That's my fucking swing!*

And it is my fucking swing.

As I speed-leaf through the feature, this becomes more and more apparent. Oh, the two guys behind it—Andy Plummer and Mike Bennett—call their thing Stack & Tilt instead of left lean, and they aren't mental health cases but established big-league coaches, and their clients aren't former fathers-in-law and first timers using their tight sweaters to cadge free lessons, but an impressive roster of Tour players. And maybe I haven't quite figured out every little aspect, but really, it's the same swing.

What an astonishing coincidence. Two centuries pass in which lots of things about the golf swing change but no-one ever says you should rotate your body around your front leg. Then, I figure it out even as a pair of big-deal teaching pros do likewise. Well done, Jeff!

Or not. After three of four seconds of manic self-congratulation, sanity returns in the form of deep depression and paralyzing self-doubt. Yesterday I'd been the inventor of a revolutionary new golf swing that seemed to work for almost everyone who gave it a chance. Today I am just another guy attempting to make a buck off an innovation that has been all but patented by these Plummer and Bennett guys.

Even if someone wants to be charitable and give me credit for coming up with it on my own, so what? There'll be plenty of other places where an aspiree can pick it up, lots of real pros who'll be only too happy to teach it.

So, woe is me. And what about poor Bill? Geez, poor Bill. Such a great guy, but what luck. First, a Saab dealership, and now this.

Well, someone has to pull things together, and for once that person will be me. "Hey buddy," I say when I walk into his office. "Bit of a kick in the gut. But it ain't over till it's over."

Suddenly I understand why so many of the manager types back at the company spoke in clichés. Given the immense gravity of their globally crucial positions, they'd convinced themselves that every sentence had to serve a purpose; that much of what they said should be plotted in advance. I didn't mean to subject poor Bill to these tired phrases, and wouldn't have ordinarily, but the creative and spontaneous part of my brain, the right side if one must, has been smothered by the left side, which has unilaterally decided that it should be mission control. It has further determined that a casual tone would be most effective, but in striving so hard to achieve this, has destroyed any possibility of truly casual unaffectedness.

"What do you mean?"

"You know, Stack & Tilt," I say, holding up the magazine. "Stack & Tilt, rip and tear." Incredibly, I make as if to tear apart the copy of *Golf Digest*.

"Oh that," says Bill. "How's your time in the next few days. Looking pretty busy."

"What do you mean? We're ruined, right?"

"Ruined? I think not. Yesterday, after I saw the magazine, I sent out a blast to my email list. 'Amazing Stack & Tilt swing as seen in *Golf Digest*! Cut strokes from your game! The first teacher on the west coast!!!'" Bill is the only person I know who can express multiple exclamation marks verbally without sounding ironic. "Not quite a thousand people on the list and I got 42 calls. I've put 18 credit cards through and I know there are another dozen who'll go for it."

Just then the phone rings, and I listen as Bill talks yet another prospective student into the $750 full meal deal. I think he even goes for the protective undercoating.

"Yeah," says Bill, after hanging up. "And you know Dan Kessler with the golf show on cable?"

"Sure, I've seen the show."

"Well, you're going to be on it. He's coming by to shoot the segment."

"*Moi*? On TV?"

"Yup. New tour swing. Local boy makes good. The producer loves it."

"So you called him?"

"Her. An old dancing partner. Kessler will be by around 6:15. I checked your schedule and you should be clear by then. It will take maybe an hour."

"Really? You know my Craigslist date? She was going to drop by at 6:30 for another lesson, then off to a movie." Like a normal person, I called Jenny back before heading for work. "But no problem, I'll move her back till later."

"You'll move her back?"

"I don't want to make her stand around waiting."

"It never crossed your mind that she might be impressed to arrive at the range and find you surrounded by a TV crew?"

"Really? That's what you'd—how you'd play it?"

"Yeah. Forty-five minutes is just the right amount of time. Much longer and she'd get bored."

"OK, I guess she won't mind."

"No. And then no more than 20 or 25 minutes on the range, right? Women won't let you close if they've been sweating."

"If you say so."

"Alcohol would help counteract that, but you've got the movie problem. What are you going to see?"

"She mentioned something. I dunno, Meg Ryan sort of thing."

"Smart of you to have her choose. And romantic comedies do work: the studios put a lot of firepower into making sure of that. Look, how important is this girl to you?"

"No big deal. She's nice."

"OK. If she were important, I'd try to get her to an art film."

"Like, from Europe?" To a cultural studies grad, this is not unfamiliar territory, but I have to confirm that the car salesmen and I are talking about the same thing.

"Lars von Trier is good. Danish. Bergman, of course. But sure, anything from Europe. Or an indie. Sundance Award Winner? Earns respect, creates a mystique. Google it first so you can say something afterward."

"And then what?" I am genuinely curious. Even I've grasped that there's some visioneering involved in the dating world, but I hadn't imagined it could be such a science.

"Look, it all depends. This isn't a science. But in general a bistro is better than a bar. There's a place called Lolita. Just opened by two young women who used to be sous chef and sommelier at Anducci's. Your date's a woman; she'll like that, right? And you say she's a journalist? Order the 100-mile tasting menu. You know, sustainability."

"I shouldn't have to ask this, but what's a tasting menu?"

"Six small dishes, one after the other. I call them foreplates."

"Heh, heh. And 100-mile?"

"All the ingredients grown within 100 miles."

"Right."

"The sommelier will recommend a 100-mile wine, of course, but it's best to temper the sensitivity with a little sophistication, so say you're feeling like something Old World. More food-friendly. Your date will appreciate the thought. Listen to the recommendations, but order off the list instead. Doing that emphasizes your masculinity."

It's becoming clear to me that working with Bill will be like having a free subscription to *Esquire*.

"If you know something about wine, order away. The 2005s should be showing up on menus now, and you can't go wrong with those, even though they will be a little fresh. You might note that. Offhandedly, of course."

"Of course."

"If you're stuck, just order something with a 'V' in it. Viognier, Grüner Veltliner, Verdicchio, Vouvray. If the lady prefers a red, ask after a Valdiguié. They won't have one, which is just fine, so order a Bordeaux blend—Cab Sauvignon *and* Petit Verdot. No Valpolicello, though."

"Why not?"

"Too checkered tablecloth, and a lot of it is crap."

"Excellent advice, Bill, but I think I'll let her choose. It's her turn to pay, too."

"God have mercy."

I've realized by now that Bill will always be two moves ahead of me, even if we aren't playing the same game. But I am grateful for the way he takes charge of Jenny when she arrives at the range only to find me occupied by Dan Kessler and his crew—the crew being a single cameraman, also responsible for sound, who manages to seem blasé and overwhelmed at the same time.

And he's the professional one. As much as Bill had briefed the producer and I'd explained everything to Kessler before the camera started rolling, he still insists on describing me as a pro, which will definitely raise some hackles, and he can't seem to accept that the swing has nothing to do with Moe Norman and Natural Golf. Eventually, I'm the one who suggests the cameraman shoot both my old and new swings from the side and behind. I also take charge of the interview, making the connection to Plummer and Bennett and *Golf Digest,* clarifying that I don't claim any Stack & Tilt certification, and providing concise and useful answers to his vague and uninformed questions. Such competence I display! How soon we forget that consecutive employers saw fit to promote me despite my many shortcomings.

And finally we are done. My handling of the situation doesn't escape Bill, or Jenny either. "Hey, you were good back there," she says.

The interview has gone overtime, and she still wants her lesson, so we decide to skip the movie and head straight to dinner, which turns out to be at a neighborhood joint where she is not only known but several of her friends have gathered. "Isn't it unusual to meet the family on the second date?" I ask.

"You forget. This isn't a date," she laughs. "Strictly platonic."

Her friends are nice: maybe a little superficial but cleverly so in the manner of journalist types. And yet the evening is a bit of a blur. My abrupt return to the working world and the day's masterful media performance seem to have drawn down the vast energy reserves I've built up during 11 months of carefully marshalling them.

Still, I try to rise to the occasion. The effort proves to be necessary, especially when I find myself talking to a guy who has been attempting to honor the historical standards of his profession with his impressive alcohol consumption. "So you teach golf," says the drunk, a city beat reporter who has headed straight across the bar to confront me.

"I guess I do."

"Good luck with that." It is clear he believes he is speaking to someone of large inheritance and small intelligence.

"How do you mean?"

"Cycles. What goes up must come down. What's that you call your swing?"

"Not my idea, but Stack & Tilt."

"Exactly. Everything has been stacked in your favor, and now it's beginning to tilt."

I look into the eyes of that rarest of human beings, someone who is even less perceptive than me. "Dude," I say after an appropriate pause.

He stares back at me, blankly.

Surely someone able to keep a job like he has cannot be an idiot, so the fault is probably mine. I have failed to complete a full sentence with the word, let alone the entire paragraphs that Dave Smart is capable of. I am confirming his opinion of my intellect. There is no choice but to elaborate. "Dude," I say. "If only you knew."

Just then Jenny arrives, halting the conversation before it can descend to previously unfathomed depths of incomprehensibility. Saved by the belle.

~ ~ ~ ~

JENNY

TV people—is there a lower form of life? Sure, Dan, here's my phone number. What girl wouldn't want to hook up with a guy who has a golf show on the community access station? So cool.

Of course, even he must score that way now and then or he wouldn't bother trying. Maybe golf is like music, with its infinitesimally gradated groupie hierarchy. You're into Oxycontin but you play drums in a death metal band? Of course I'd like to hang out in your van. Gotta start somewhere.

And Dan, you're so dumb you made the sound guy look smart, but you played on the golf team at your two-year college? Sure, we can get together later. Just give me a half-hour to get rid of this other dude, who teaches at the driving range. Then, after I tag along with you for a while, maybe I'll meet a guy who's almost good enough for the whatchamacallit Nationwide Tour. Yeah, I'll just keep climbing that ladder, all the way up to Tiger Woods.

Maybe there's an article there. I'll go undercover. Infiltrate Tiger's camp. Play the temptress and see if he'll bite. What, he's married? To a Swedish model? Well, sure the odds are long, but that just makes it a bigger story.

I suppose I am undercover, in a way. I wish Jeff wasn't such a sweet guy. Strange, yes. But sweet. Jenny Spencer, you are hereby making a solemn pledge to do everything possible to avoid harming this completely decent fellow. Maybe you can even help him. Starting right now, since he seems to be talking to Harrison, and that's a conversation that can only ever be awkward. Over we go to launch the rescue operation.

CHAPTER 4
THE TERRIBLE NOISE

JEFF, MAY 27, 2007

Rolling into the office sharp at 9:54, I find myself wondering what the morning crisis or excuse for champagne might be, but it seems that after less than three weeks the business has entered its mature phase, in which challenges are proficiently dealt with and opportunities efficiently exploited. Bill begins the daily briefing by telling me not to worry about the Dan Kessler situation. A call to the producer friend confirmed that the on-air talent comes cheap and is at best a deep-voiced idiot, but the production company spends its money on a crack editor who will be in touch before rewriting the script and turning Kessler's inept interview into a respectable segment of the sort we are familiar with.

Meanwhile, Bill continues to field inquiries from prospective Stack & Tilters, and is successful in signing up an appropriate proportion. He is revising the business plan accordingly, and I will be able to start drawing a full salary next month, well ahead of schedule. In other words, ho-hum: another day making decent money doing something you love. Fortunately, my personal life shows every sign of stepping in to ensure cause aplenty for any facial tics I might suffer.

Chief among the issues, in just over a month my mother is due in town, as is—either less or more ominously, it's just too hard to predict—my father. Who knows how the weekend will go? I envision one part manic *I Love Lucy*, two parts cringe-inducing *Curb Your Enthusiasm*. It will be up to me and my enhanced mental health to make sure there is no *Throw Momma From The Train*.

Of equally portentous note, it appears I might be juggling two women on the reunion weekend. Jenny and I are getting together pretty much every second evening, and on the most recent occasion a couple of interesting things occurred. Number 1, she began to hit the ball rather well. On our first meeting I assessed her athletic ability as pretty average, but either I misjudged her or golf isn't a sport, as various know-nothings are foolish enough to maintain. Because, wow: she hit some pretty solid shots and looked ready to head out on an executive course, as I promised we'd shortly do.

She was charged up and so was I, which might have played a role in how the goodnight kiss played out. "Plato would not approve, even at his retreat!" she said after we disentangled from a teenage-style clasp, somehow engaged in from our respective seats in the Neon—another clue to her latent athleticism, come to think of it. I don't know what got into me but I patted her on the ass after I walked her to the door of the apartment building, and I don't know what got into her but she ground her ass right back into my hand and indeed into me. "Now behave," she laughed before smooching me on the cheek and disappearing inside the lobby. I speculated afterward that perhaps flirtatious behavior and a gradual escalation of sexual intimacy is a culturally determined norm and not the Hollywood fantasy I have always assumed. In any case she is scheduled to join us at the restaurant on the epochal Friday night after sire, dam and progeny spend some time sizing each other up.

To another man it would perhaps seem strange that planning has reached such an advanced stage after barely a week and with several weeks still to go. But another man would not have consented to allowing his mother to make all the preparations, and if he had, the mother would not have been mine. Since that first phone call, we have spoken several times, and a few things have become clearer, if not about her and me, then at least about the current predicament. Apparently Hector tracked her down using the miracle of Google. All he had was her name from the long ago note, but he got a hit when a Hiroshi Nakamura popped up as an attendee at some science conference and took it from there. Mom retired early from her job at a lab affiliated with my cherished alma mater and moved out of town to an adult recreational community of the type I was once complicit in creating, and there she is now pursuing a new set of crypto-scientific obsessions. I'm not the sort to cut out cartoons and tack them up—that would indicate an eagerness to engage with the world and a willing embrace of a certain brand of nerdiness—but perhaps it is a measure of the new me that I have in fact done exactly that. There it is, beside the telephone: a drawing by someone named Nick Kim showing a classroom scene in which the students are holding all manner of strange beasts and the inscription "Genetic Engineering 101" is chalked on the blackboard. "OK," the professor is saying. "Is there anyone else whose homework ate their dog?"

The strange thing is, some of Mom's ideas are actually beginning to make sense. Apparently she is something of a pioneer in the study of a field called tissue morphogenesis, which even scientists of the sane and reputable variety look to as an explanation for why evolutionary change seems to occur more jerkily than Darwin and his intellectual descendants theorized. Sometimes it's hard for me to judge whether the antipathy I feel toward her is a reasonable response or symptomatic of a tendency to overreact, as apparently I am capable of doing.

This is a question I even broached with Syd, who dodged an honest answer by saying that we are both nuts. The thing with Syd is weird to say the least: although the relationship has been strictly telephonic, she and I seem to get on as easily as ever, without any of the anger and suspicion one would expect of people who've been through such a pipeline explosion. She wants to help out in the hosting department, partly because, knowing my mom and me, she understands that help will be needed, and partly because she's just damn curious to meet my dad. Finding the time is going to be difficult, since at partner Bob's behest, she signed up to help out at the Gay Games on the same weekend. But the plan is she'll join us on the Saturday, when we'll disrupt yet another restaurant with our familial antics, or so I fear. How can it be otherwise? Into a clearly stressful situation, fate will be throwing me, the sometimes catatonic and always self-flagellating misanthrope, and my mom, the dragon lady whose focus is as intense as it is misdirected. As for Hector, who knows, but everyone has a neurotic tendency of some sort. What if he's, say, a narcissist? There we'll be in the restaurant, mom remonstrating, me simmering and Hector preening. In envisioning the weekend as a dark comedy rather than the opening scene in a police procedural, perhaps I've been too optimistic.

To my considerable surprise I also find myself continuing to share my apprehensions with Bill, who has taken on an advisory role. "You didn't have the parent problems, did you?" I ask him.

"No, my sisters and I referred to our family as the Waltonsons. Mom and dad were down at the store most of the time, so we had a lot of freedom, but also a lot of responsibility: that's the Scandinavian way."

"What would the Scandinavian approach be to reconciling with your control freak mother at exactly the same time as you were seeing your father for the first time?"

"Choose somewhere with high ceilings and simple straight-forward architecture. That will encourage civility and directness."

He says this with a straight face, then looks at me to check out my reaction. What a card. "No, seriously, you just have to be big about it. Your mother's a case, you say. Then it's your job to be the sane one. Your dad is doing something courageous, but he's the one in a foreign country, reaching out to people he knows nothing about. You have to make it comfortable for him."

Me as the mature and balanced one, that would mark a sharp break with recent reality. But I do have it in me. And dammit, I resolve, that will be the Jeff Jones on display on at least one weekend this year.

As for the weekend upcoming, I hope the Jeff Jones on display will be the one who hits high yet piercing 4-irons that bite into the green like javelin tips before dancing up to the pin. Because, yes, I am entering a biggish local tournament. Bill and I agreed from the start that this would be part of the business plan, but at the time I'd thought the rationale was to get the word out, to play offence. Now I can see that there will also be some defence involved: playing well might or might not be good for business, but playing poorly will almost certainly be bad.

The realization has been sparked by a conversation with one of my students. Most of these conform to a certain type: the deeply committed golfer who doesn't play as well as he thinks he should and thus is vulnerable to every new training aid or swing wrinkle that comes along. Bill told me this would be the case and I shouldn't worry about exploiting their vulnerability—that I would be serving the same important purpose as holistic cancer cures and organized religion.

This was Bill being sardonic, his point being that the important thing is for students to believe that someone is looking out for them; any improvement in their games is just a nice bonus. Pretty much the pedagogical approach one would expect from a Saab salesman.

That said, it's also the case that for Bill religion is more than just a multi-purpose metaphor waiting in the parts bin. In fact, he is a flat-out atheist who has developed a thorough refutation of spirituality in general, and even something of a counter-faith, which he terms "responsible hedonism." A drinker and wine guy, he initially struggled to rationalize the five percent or so of his income that always seemed to go for alcohol, he told me. But the three or four glasses of wine he consumes every day contribute to the happiness and well-being of both him and others, he has come to believe. And if he blows off a few thousand dollars a year in the process, is that any different from what religionists (as he calls them) spend in pursuit of the same end? Perhaps a tiny fraction of the money collected at their places of worship is devoted to good deeds, but the vast majority goes to keeping the lights on and the staff paid, just like a bar or winery. Meanwhile, a chunk of his alcohol expenditure is gathered up as taxes by the state, which admittedly fails to support a social safety net of Scandinavian quality, but still.

"By the way," he said. "Did you know that only five percent of Danes regularly attend church?"

"Really?"

"Yeah, compared to 44 percent of Americans."

There are other aspects to Bill's canon: the scientifically proven longer life spans and lower morbidity of moderate drinkers; their propensity to make more money and thus pay higher taxes and die with bigger estates, which can then be bequeathed to charities; the rich history and deep cultural importance of alcohol (arguably the equal of religion, Bill maintains, at least in northern Europe); drink's complete and utter innocence as a cause of war and genocide. These and other factors easily outweigh any deleterious effects, in his estimation. Yes, some five to 10 percent of the population is prone to problem drinking and must be managed, but wouldn't many of these have fallen by the wayside, in any case? In Muslim countries, the proportion of the population damaged in some way is scarcely lower. Best to drink up and live large during your utterly finite life—a sentiment I can't really disagree with, even if I can't pull it off.

My student on the range insists that I do a fair bit of ball-striking, which makes little sense, realistically. It would take an eye much more discerning than his to detect the distinctions between my swing and the modern norm, and he doesn't watch the swing anyway, instead letting himself be distracted by the flight of the ball. It's a phenomenon I am becoming accustomed to. These 15 and 25 handicappers need proof that someone at least can make the thing work. If they can't bring their own caps down a couple of strokes, so be it, as long as they haven't hitched their wagons to a loser instructor with a loser swing.

"So Kevin, I want you to take your normal stance."

"Did you intentionally hit a fade or was that a mis-hit?"

"A fade, but it cut a touch more than I wanted."

"What's your index?"

"I've haven't been playing much while I worked on the swing change," I say, somewhat truthfully. "But now I think I'd be around scratch, maybe even a plus. Shot a 70 from the back tees at Dunbar a couple of weeks ago."

"Nice. What were you before?"

"Three or four," I lie. Students like Kevin want to know that the swing has lowered my handicap but they aren't likely to buy that it cut off five or six strokes unless I also tell them about the 11 months of seven-hour days spent on the range—and a recent history involving clinical insanity and deeply antisocial behavior just isn't good for business.

That brilliant insight I owe in part to Jenny, who by now knows a fair bit about my personal situation. "Can and will be used against you," is pretty much her mantra, based on her journalism experience. She's been in the business for a decade and has more than paid her dues, she feels. Coming out of school, she spent several years at community newspapers until she got tired of being forever the second fiddle, journalistically speaking, and left for freelance writing and editing, mostly for a company with a batch of local and regional magazines. "If I were two inches taller and five percent hotter, I'd have the big newspaper job," she told me one day on the putting green. At 5' 4" or so, she isn't exactly tiny, and with her blue eyes, perky features and curvy figure, she's anything but hard on the eyes, so even I knew to protest that she looks great.

"Well, whatever," she said. "But I'm ready for something good to happen."

As it is she writes articles for the company's various magazines and websites—forestry, agriculture, mining, real estate, whatever. If nothing else, it gives her lots of things to talk about. "Did you know that placer mines are the perfect cover for marijuana grow-ops?" she asked me one day, while she was hitting balls and I was checking to make sure her ass was in ideal alignment.

I wasn't even sure what a placer mine is, though my guess that it is a way of getting gold from a river was essentially correct. "Think about it," she said. "You're at a remote location, and heavy security is the historically appropriate norm. You're expected to have a diesel generator and a couple of industrial buildings inside that razor wire fence, and to pay your bills in cash. Until the price of gold started inching up a couple of years ago, it was pretty much impossible to make money *except* by growing pot."

No, she hadn't exactly swept me off my feet, nor I off hers, but we like each other and the relationship is definitely progressing. It doesn't hurt that she is happy to soak up as much golf knowledge as she can. Rules, handicaps, design aspects, the business side: she is interested in everything, which is to be expected of a journalist, I guess. When I told her the tournament I was playing in was at a new quasi-minimalist course, she asked what the hell I was talking about and wanted to know all about it.

I wouldn't ordinarily embark on an explication of the history of golf course design, but she'd just told me about placer mines and Wwoofers, which—who knew?—are volunteers who trade labour for accommodation at organic farms, so on I plunged, checking carefully every few sentences to make sure I wasn't becoming more of a bore than usual.

"You've probably never heard of Bandon Dunes," I said, "but to a golfer, it's Coach to Pebble Beach's Hermes." I hope I had the analogy right. In truth Coach had me a little confused. I've heard the expression "Coach is for women who ride coach," which I suppose is a putdown, and I'm a fan of Bandon Dunes, so I didn't want that. Then again, is that truly the case or just an easy metaphor chanced upon by a snobbish spa receptionist? A guy absorbs a certain amount of fashion context, but you can never truly understand. And anyway, I decided, how many people would be able to call me on an errant golf design/handbag metaphor?

"There are three courses there now, but when the first one opened a few years ago, it pretty much changed the entire golf landscape." At the company, knowing about this stuff was practically a professional responsibility, so I didn't have to feel too geeky about delving further back into golf design lore. "Until the 1950s courses were laid out on the landscape pretty much as it sat because moving dirt was so expensive. Fortunately, there was lots of land around, so usually they ended up on a patch that worked for golf; if not, the better designers got pretty good at playing with the subtleties, while the poorer ones gave us some pretty crappy tracks—most of which are long gone or renovated beyond recognition anyway. Nowadays the era that ended around then is known as the Golden Age of Golf Design."

I checked her over for level of interest. Her eyes still seemed bright enough, but I decided to go for another metaphor, one in keeping with her nascent interest in design, sparked because she was starting to write stories on residential architecture for one of the company's magazines. "In architectural terms think of it as mid-century modernism: designed rather than decorated, straight to the point, timeless, elegant.

"But then a bunch of things happened: new machinery made it cheaper to move dirt, good land got more and more scarce, people got used to paying more to play, and then, to top it all off, some ass-hat invented the golf course community."

Jenny knows about this aspect of my sordid past so she smiled in an appropriate manner.

"Meanwhile, glamorous stars like Jack Nicklaus and Arnold Palmer brought a whole new crowd to the game—younger guys with better equipment who could hit the ball a long way. They couldn't be given wide fairways to pound their drivers down, not when only the tough courses were getting any cred. Everyone wanted to feel challenged, after all—as if they were playing a Tour venue like the ones they saw on their new color TVs. Of course, that also meant the courses had to be highly manicured and very predictable. If you made a good shot, you had to be rewarded; bad bounces wouldn't do."

She still seemed interested, so no strained comparison to padded shoulders or other dated fashion elements.

"The solution was to landscape like mad, moving tons and tons of dirt so that everything was nice and smooth. Then they laid out rows of big, ugly bunkers along the edge of the fairways. This was partly to frame the holes visually—to show you what you were supposed to do—and partly to punish you if you failed to do it.

"How patriarchal."

"Indeed." As a lapsed cultural studier, I knew exactly what the lapsed feminist was talking about. "But what truly characterized the Dark Ages is water. Not only were water hazards a course's primary defence against low scores, they looked good from the houses that crowded against the fairways. And the dirt dug out to make the ponds provided the fill for the houses to sit on. By the end of the 1980s, that was the norm: houses lining every hole and water, water everywhere."

"With fountains," Jenny said brightly.

"Yes, those were pretty much the last straw," I said. "But at least they were vaguely functional for aerating the water—unlike waterfalls." Regrettably, my tenure at the company came during the great millennial waterfall fad, and we were careful to install one every chance we got.

"Anyway, those were the awful Eighties," I concluded. "Artificial-looking holes with too much water and dozens of big bunkers in all the right—and therefore wrong—places. Houses crowding in from all sides. And a design philosophy based on rewarding a perfect shot and punishing a bad one while leaving little room for strategy or serendipity."

"It all sounds rather severe."

"And ugly. But what came along in the 1990s?"

"Uh, Bandon Dunes?"

"Right, grunge golf."

I decided not to complicate my pop history with Pete Dye and the gradual growth of consciousness that he helped spark, or with Bandon's minimalist predecessors, like the revered Coore/Crenshaw's Sand Dunes in Nebraska. That course is like Antarctica anyway. Ninety-nine point nine percent of us will never see it, and can only trust that it exists. No doubt there is a website for conspiracy theorists convinced that it doesn't.

No, better to keep things nice and tidy. "This guy named Mike Keiser, who'd made a fortune with a line of humorous greeting cards, went to Scotland and discovered that it's an entirely different game over there. He found a derelict property right on the coast and brought in a young Scottish designer who went straight back to the roots—no houses, no water, no trees that weren't already growing; no power carts or paths, and the whole thing planted to fescue fairways and greens that played firm and fast. Pretty much like the Old Country."

"And now all the cool new courses are like that," she inferred.

"Sadly, no. A lot of them invoke the idea of links courses for marketing purposes, but not many play that way. Most of them still have soft greens, so you can fly your ball on and stick it American-style—and they're guarded in front so that you have to. I tried to push our courses further toward minimalism, but there was a lot of resistance."

"Why?"

"The usual. Designers who like things the way they've always been, greenskeepers resistant to new turfs, golf guys afraid the customers won't like it: stodgaholics in general. And let's not forget the bean counters with no imagination and the marketing VPs with no principles."

That came out of nowhere, and Jenny gave me a little look before laughing it off. I'd striven to give her only the barest outline of my marital troubles, but one evening, during an unguarded moment facilitated by a bottle of Verdicchio—thank you, Bill—I'd let slip something about Kevin. The new me is becoming a bit of a Chatty Cathy.

She sidled over and put her arm around my back. "Ah, a whole year and poor baby still can't get over it."

"I'm over it," I said. "Onwards and upwards!"

"Right. You go, sport," she said.

~ ~ ~ ~

JEFF, JUNE 2

The Saturday morning of the tournament the Neon is going through one of its periodic coughing fits—VT, Bill calls it: vehicular tuberculosis. For a time I worry it isn't going to get me there. As it is, I pull in only a half hour before my tee time with hardly any time to loosen up on the range.

After discussions yesterday that took the better part of an hour, it's been determined that I will be playing as a pro. I don't have any kind of PGA certification, but I am making money from the game, and that, it became clear, renders me a professional.

Realistically, I'm thrilled. How often does 11 months of obsessive-compulsive dysfunction lead to a satisfying and reasonably remunerative new career? In this tournament the pros and scratch or near-scratch amateurs are playing together anyway, but a good finish as an amateur might net me a new golf bag, while for the newly christened pro, there could be hundreds of dollars—or heck, maybe even thousands.

Shaking hands on the tee box I'm mildly awed by the youth of the two college players in the group, but it is their drives that truly stun me. We have some long hitters at Dunbar, but these guys just crush the ball. Jesse and Colin will both be hitting wedges to a pin that's 445 yards away, while fellow-pro Carl and I figure to need mid-irons after our wimpy 270-yard tee shots. How can we compete?

But not to fret. We make for a pleasant foursome, and surprisingly well-matched too. The young college guys suffer a few loose swings, and Carl's short game is a little rusty. Not too many teaching pros can draw upon 25,000 recent hours of reps, apparently. If anyone notices my nonconformist swing, they don't say anything, but they can't help but comment on my steady play, marred only by a couple of three-putts on the unfamiliar and roly-poly greens. On the scorecard I end up low man with a 68; indeed, as the last groups come in, it seems more and more apparent that I will be playing in the final foursome on Sunday. Trapped amidst the typical clubhouse bonhomie, I begin to experience familiar feelings of social discomfort as my cherished anonymity gradually gives way to a decidedly uncherished identity, that of a mysterious sandbagger.

Or so it goes till the clock strikes three, and the giant-screen TV is switched away from the weekend Tour stop to—what's this, a cable station? But, of course. It's time for none other than that local golf institution, the Dan Kessler show. And what should the first segment concern but the radical new Stack & Tilt swing and, more specifically, the seemingly personable and well-adjusted person who's teaching it at the Tivoli Golf and Learning Center.

"Hey, turn that up," someone says, having made the connection between the face on the TV and the face in the lounge. Conversation ceases as everyone watches me going through an exaggerated demonstration of the differences between my take on Stack & Tilt and the regular swing.

"So, you're the guy," someone says, less than brilliantly. "I've been hearing about that. You really think it works?"

"I think it works for me," I say, sensing a hint of the hostility that seems to afflict a lot of teaching pros when it comes to Stack & Tilt—apparently Bill wasn't exaggerating when he said that some would finger it is a cause of cancer. "And I guess I've had some success with my students."

"You were, what, net 64 today? I guess it does work," he says, to considerable laughter.

"I took a year off while I worked on the swing," I say, attempting to diffuse the sandbag talk.

"After tomorrow, you'll know all about it," says Matt from the club, jumping to my aid. "I took a lesson from him, and it's the real deal." A few minutes of civil discussion ensues, before I drink up and go home. All things considered, maybe it's all for the good. The clubhouse cynics have been at least partially disarmed. And hey, if you're going to be playing in the final group, better to be the guy who's stealing money from the pros with his great play than an amateur who's cheating on his handicap.

~ ~ ~ ~

JEFF, JUNE 3

Sunday dawns bright and clear. And dark and rainy. And there is an ice storm. And then, at 3:32, I bolt awake.

Well, no worries. The pros are famous for playing well on the weekend despite being unable to sleep the night before, and who can doubt that Jeff Jones, recent basket case, has as much gumption as they?

The several hours left to kill do bring up an issue that has begun to concern me, however. With golf rapidly becoming my vocation, it will perhaps be wise to find an avocation, given that every teaching pro I have ever known seems happy to do almost anything other than play the game they make their living at. But what?

Reading doesn't seem to work for me anymore. In college I consumed all the usual undergrad novels, and now and then even experienced that *Catcher In The Rye* moment when it seems that someone has tapped into your inner soul. Apparently, go figure, I am attracted to characters who exist almost entirely within their own heads. But living with Syd I fell out of the reading habit, somehow finding the 25 hours a week we devoted to sex and golf more satisfying than an imaginary character's startling insights and paralysing self-analysis.

Meanwhile, I am worse than inept when it comes to working with my hands. Plus, I have some Bill-like, quasi-religious philosophies of my own. These boil down to no power tools and no measuring devices, a belief system that Syd pegged as aligning me with the Amish. I never consciously decided that measuring something or triggering an electric motor is immoral, of course. It's more a case of faint personal preferences becoming ingrained over time. Arguably, I've been spared a certain amount of harm as a result. Just as strictures against beef helped keep the Hindus from eating themselves out of dairy products and not consuming pork saved the Muslims from Trichinosis, my eccentricities helped me escape unpleasant consequences such as fixing the garden shed and vacuuming the living room.

Then again, what good is labour avoidance if there's nothing else to fill the time with? It's now 4:05, six hours before my tee time and a good four hours before even Vijay Singh would head to the practice range. Idly I start playing on the laptop, pursuing the activity known as "surfing," which must have seemed a fresh and invigorating description when it was coined.

The first interlude is mostly devoted to golf and real estate, a function, I suppose, of the interest the course has piqued. Garry Oaks—named in honour of the gnarliest tree in creation and a common species in these parts—is the work of one of our smaller competitors, a firm that does seem to know how to build a golf course, even if it isn't so hot at selling the real estate. Or so it would seem. The course has been open for a couple of years, but there's barely a house to be seen on the empty cul-de-sacs around it.

Checking out the website I see that, sure enough, probably 90 percent of the lots are still for sale, and there has even been a round of price reductions. Hard to believe, given the roaring market of the past few years. The situation recently caught the notice of a local business publication, which reports a similar situation at other developments, even one of ours.

During my time at the company, selling lots was the least of our worries. Getting them to market as quickly as possible; blending in the inexpensive tweaks and features that would ensure we got top dollar (hello, waterfalls): those were the imperatives.

At first a lot of our projects were in glamor destinations: the Aspens and Whistlers of the world. But the company was one of the first to recognize how difficult it is to get anything done in places like those. Land is expensive, regulations are stringent and the nimbyism is profound. Sure, bond fund managers and dot. com nouveau rich-ers who got their money out in the nick of time would stumble along to pay $5 million for the timber-frame monstrosities that eventually got built, but what a production!

So we searched for new frontiers. Colorado mountain resorts a gong show? Well hey, over by the Utah border there's a plateau with beautiful mountain views, cheap ranchland and local councils who'd love to get in on some of the development action. Put in a nice golf course and suddenly a dusty whistlestop like Montrose or Grand Junction looks pretty good to all those Freedom-55ers from Peoria and Winnebraska who aren't made of money and don't ski anyway. For a time I served as one of our advance scouts, crisscrossing the arid plateaus that separate the majestic mountains from the pounding Pacific, because it was there that the action was moving, or so we hoped. Too many low-lifes in Vegas? Welcome to Mesquite. Tahoe not your cup of herbal tea? Ladies and gentlemen, get a taste of Bend. Kelowna out of your provincial tax bracket? Behold Kamloops!

But now when I look at how some of the developments are doing, the picture seems not quite so bright. Three years in, the course open and Phase 1 still not sold out? That couldn't be a good thing for old Kevin. And when I check on Zillow, real estate values in some places actually seem to be going down.

Crazy: Since peaking a year earlier, prices in Mesquite have dropped nine percent. Even crazier, in June 2006 the average house price in Bend was $383,000, and now, a year later, it's $335,000. The graph looks like the ski slope those Tahoe refuse-niks decided to pass up in favor of an isolated town with a volca-no inside the city limits. It's an extinct volcano, but still—that's some kind of ominous metaphor.

Well, no big deal in the scheme of things, I suppose. The company is large enough that we subscribed to an economic forecasting service, and I read enough reports to know the big picture. The economy isn't quite post-cyclical, as Greenspan seemed to think, but even if there were a downturn, the currents supporting the kind of housing we provided are just so strong: a technological revolution that allows people to work from their back decks; all those baby-boomer early retirees with their fat home equities and juicy stock portfolios; the inexorable transfor-mation from a society defined by work to one defined by lifestyle. With so many developers onto this and money so easy to come by, the supply of homes sometimes outraces demand, but things will balance out. All in all, it's pretty hard to imagine that places like Bend and Mesquite won't bounce right back from their year in the real estate wilderness.

Oh sure, on the web there are a few dissenting voices arguing otherwise. There are always Cassandras. At the company I sometimes worked alongside a landsman of the radical right-wing persuasion, a guy in his 50s named Bob Flecks. Goldbug, conspiracy theorist, wacko fundamentalist, closet racist—the whole package. A pleasant enough guy who had nothing against me personally, but gather three or four of us Asian/African/Latino crossbreds on a street corner and you know there would be mumblings at his chapter of the John Birch Society, or whatever they call themselves these days. No doubt he had a cabin in the woods with a concealed trap door leading to the guns and canned goods.

At the same time I somehow manage to stay in contact with a couple of guys from my cultural studies days. Swinging from the left rather than the right, they nevertheless share many of Flecks' traits and even some of his views. Although comfortably ensconced in academia, they remain convinced that the world is going to hell in a handcart and hopeful that people like me, the kind who build and populate golf course communities, are as doomed as the heinous world view we espouse.

In my most recent conversation with good old Trevor Vestich, I actually owned up to the incident with Kevin, admitting that not only had I incinerated his Porsche, I'd then broken into his place and pissed all over his stuff. Maybe I was looking for a little street cred. A self-styled anarchist, Trev had once been a member of the so-called Black Bloc, and even suited up for the Battle in Seattle, though he would have been, good lord, in his 30s by then. He found my tale amusing, of course, but also, he claimed, a little disquieting. Oh, torching a Porsche was pretty cool. But apparently I once told him I'd never live on a golf course because that was only for the rare subset of people whose thing is watching men pee—and two urine references from the same person rang some sort of warning bell with him. "Hey," he said. "Whatever works for you—but watersports?"

Well, always the critic. By now it's 6:22, and by stretching out the morning routine I can arrive at the course an hour and a half before my tee time, which will be just about right. One last quick exercise before I turn off the computer, though. I stuck around long enough yesterday to know who I'll be playing with, so I can search their names and see what comes up.

Preston Stiglitz: Now there's a guy who won't need any numerals in his gmail address. Also someone whose name is familiar to me: a local pro who played on the Nike Tour for a season or two and now teaches out of the local munis. He obviously keeps his game in shape because he's a frequent contender at tournaments.

Jason Wong: A "pro in training," as we savvy golf insiders term the best of the college players. This local-boy-making-good won an NCAA tournament in February, which vaulted him to 424 in the Royal and Ancient's World Amateur rankings. Although not extra long by college standards, he'll still leave me 20 yards behind off the tee.

Farley Stinson: Another gmail lottery winner and, what's this, a natural golfer? The Moe Norman swing didn't catch on with a lot of people. It's hard to work the ball, and the distance penalty figures to be getting worse by the year, but here's a guy who can obviously get it done. At Dunbar we have a natural golfer, and playing with him is always a hoot: like watching golf as conducted in one of Bill's parallel universes.

It figured to be an interesting group, and so it proves to be. What a contrast in styles as we play the 440-yard first. On paper Wong and Stiglitz seemed the most similar, but that's not the way it turns out. In the contemporary manner Wong flights his ball high in the air, relying more on trajectory than spin to stop it on the greens. Stiglitz is a throwback to the days of persimmon drivers, when a lot of the best players slung out low draws that scorched along only a few feet off the ground like cruise missiles flying under the radar. As expected Stinson is the shortest among us, but not by much. A big guy, he can get his drive out 280 and more, so the distance penalty isn't significant. We all reach in regulation, and Stinson, of all people, sinks his 15-footer. Maybe someone ahead of us will shoot a 64, rendering anything our group pulls off irrelevant, but inside our little bubble the four of us are playing with our eyes on the prize, which happens to be eight grand for first place—real money for those of us able to take it.

And let it be said that each of us rises to the occasion. Finally, on the ninth, the usually straight-hitting Stinson inexplicably pushes his drive OB, setting him up for a triple. That leaves three of us within a stroke of each other, with another stroke separating us from anyone in the foursomes ahead, as we discover at the turn. I've been in pressure situations at the club, and generally acquitted myself well, to the surprise of everyone, I'm sure. True, the stakes are higher here, but in the past I never had an Oldsmobile to park around the course. And now it's not just any Oldsmobile—certainly not a mere Cutlass Supreme with Landau roof, which I've abandoned as too large for my purposes. Now I am aiming at a mid-1970s Starfire, a badge-engineered derivative of the Chevy Vega that most people have wiped from their consciousness in what might be a rare legitimate case of repressed memory syndrome.

Yes, that's how precise my shotmaking is. There's no need to scramble and barely even any to putt when almost every shot bounces off the signature aluminum band dissecting the Starfire's tinted-glass Astroroof. Indeed, as bad a car as the Starfire indisputably was, I find it considerably more appealing than the Cutlass. The Chevy Vega may have been a complete dog, but it was a good-looking dog, and the 2+2 Starfire and its ilk were whittled from that car with the Ferrari 365 in mind. The GM stylists didn't quite nail it, needless to say, but the fastback coupe they came up with was still a tidy design and one of the better looking cars to emerge from Detroit over the past few decades. One doesn't want to get too Bob Rotella-ish, but perhaps the intellectual bankruptcy exemplified by the Cutlass could constitute a portal for negative thoughts to enter the golfer's head. Perhaps too, it makes sense not to be stuffing said head with visions of an object that mocks one's cherished belief that form follows function, the modernist creed. On the other hand, is it truly wise to ally myself with a lovable loser instead of a vehicle that perfected the art of winning ugly?

These are my thoughts as I walk down the par-5 17th. Golf psychologists like Rotella are divided on whether it's better to focus the mind on the game or to achieve a relaxed, almost meditative state, as I seem to be doing with my musings on the esthetic merits of General Motors vehicles from the 1970s and '80s and their larger significance as symbols of the dominant North American culture. Well, something is working, because form and function are in ideal alignment in the case of this mulatto ball-striker. With four birdies in the past five holes, I hold a two-stroke lead on Wong and Stiglitz, and am coming around to the idea that two more pars will win me an $8,000 check.

Consequently, looking at 250 yards to a green hanging above a gully and tightly guarded with bunkers in front, I decide to lay up to 80 yards—smooth 60-degree wedge—with my second. Stiglitz does much the same, while Wong, of course, goes for it from 235, managing to hold the back right fringe for an almost certain birdie. Stiglitz and I both wedge inside 15 feet, but I miss high, while he makes and Wong two-putts, cutting my lead over the two of them to one stroke.

The dogleg-right 18th at Garry Oaks is a beauty, playing through a barely disturbed swath of the original oaks ecosystem. The trees are very much an issue, and the designer managed to retain big patches of native meadow, which just weeks ago would have been lushly carpeted with camas lilies.

Wong, playing that high trajectory of his, could easily cut the corner, leaving a short-iron to the green, even though it's 470 yards away. Meanwhile, Stiglitz, with his low draw, will be forced to take the long way around, making it more like driver, 4-iron. I'm in between the two, and not certain what line I should take. I can flight my driver almost as high as Wong can, but my carry tops out around 275 compared to his 290, and that will give me a different landing area, with less fairway and more meadow. Then again, even though I've been striking the ball beautifully, I have put a few into that sort of rough and found it to be quite amenable; meanwhile, the greens are playing pretty firm and the well-bunkered complex on 18 is no picnic for someone approaching with a long iron. So, after watching Wong power fade a monster to maybe 140, I decide to try a similar shot, hoping to nail the thin ribbon of fairway 160 yards or so from the pin but content to take my chances if I find the rough instead.

It's perhaps a minor flaw of my routine that in situations like this, where the landing area isn't visible, I require a slightly different visualization process. I put the flashers on in the Oldsmobile and watch them blinking through the trees. Nevertheless, I am confident as I step up to the tee, and confident too as I follow the flight of the ball. It stays pretty straight instead of fading, but at worst that will bounce me through the fairway into light rough. And so it proves to be. With a good lie and 160 yards to the pin, all I need to do is hit a smooth 8-iron to the safe part of the green, trusting that a two-putt for 68 will be enough to beat the other two, who will have to birdie one of the toughest holes on the course, even to tie.

Walking down the fairway my thoughts are concentrated on the respective hood ornaments of the Starfire and Cutlass Supreme. During the mid-1980s the Cutlass featured a unit that was only mildly objectionable: a chrome rectangle framing a silver and red shield adapted from an "authentic" early-20th century Oldsmobile logo variation. Yes, it was so typical of the era that a "classic" design would be updated in an attempt to play to heritage, that excuse for banality and stodginess so deeply embraced by Middle America. I guess in a consumer society, that's the form that ancestor worship takes. Still, the execution or the ornament was respectable from a graphic design point of view, so I would have to cut it some slack.

And would the Starfire even have a hood ornament? I don't have the answer, but suspect not, at least not of the protruding variety. In fact, the use of chrome brightwork was in gradual decline during the 1960s and '70s, a reaction to the excesses of the 1950s. But around 1970 America discovered Mercedes and its deservedly iconic three-pointed star. Most European marques got along just fine without freestanding hood ornaments, but Audis, BMWs, Alfas and the like failed to capture the New World imagination in quite the same way, and perhaps this was due to a lack of prominent radiator-style grilles, a vestigial feature that car buyers can't seem to get away from even today.

Back when he was dealing Saabs, Bill had been inordinately concerned about such things, and one day he laid out the hood ornament situation in considerable detail. Ralph Nader types first began to question the safety of protruding ornaments in the 1960s, eventually leading to legislation in 1973; many companies simply did away with them in favor of tidy badges or other solutions. Mercedes, however, felt the star was a crucial part of its identity and instead solved the problem by engineering a spring-loaded ornament. These were an instant hit and, although prone to theft and vandalism, not only boosted the company's reputation but convinced others that they too needed spring-loaded units. Bill suspects their popularity may even have been a factor in the rise of so-called formal styling, which reached its zenith in the 1970s with the profusion of opera windows and padded vinyl roofs. But the Starfire was an inexpensive subcompact that wasn't intended to look like a Mercedes but rather, well, a Ferrari. It might have escaped the hood-ornament plague.

With this in mind and 8-iron in hand, I decide to eschew the Astroroof in favor of the spot on the hood where I hope a mere badge will be. Wise choice. My shot lands exactly where I want it, on almost the only place that allows me to stay safe yet stop within 30 feet of the pin. Meanwhile, Stiglitz has got himself into trouble and will have to scramble for a par, while Wong will be putting for birdie but is outside me.

Could winning a tournament of this caliber really be so painless? There is quite a gallery encircling the green, certainly the largest I've ever played in front of. Many of the players from earlier foursomes have trooped out to watch, and friends and family are also in attendance. I'm gratified to see both Bill and Jenny standing behind the green, and happy as well that there's no sign of Syd. She is unaware of Jenny, and this is not the moment to be plotting introductions. Also, given recent skirt incidents, there's the possibility she'd feel I am in need of bucking up and decide to deploy the magic vagina. Better to train my thoughts on hood ornaments, thank you very much.

Stinson and even Stiglitz are not in contention now, and graciously attempt to stay out of the way while holing out their longer putts. Wong is up before me, of course, with an almost perfectly straight uphiller that he's unlikely to leave short. He's played quickly all day, but this one he studies from all directions, rehearsing the stroke a couple of times before stepping up to address the ball. He sends it on a line maybe six inches right of the hole, expecting it to bend back, but that's not what happens. It even fades a touch further right, leaving him a tap-in from a foot or so, promptly accomplished.

Now it's my turn to step up, a signal for the gallery to hush. I've had lots of time to study the line, and figure that right edge will do it. The plan is to die the ball into the hole instead of running it a couple of feet past, as I would normally do. I don't need a birdie, after all, only a two-putt. Back goes the putter head, and now the ball is rolling. Not too fast, not too slow, just right, and precisely center cup. Alas, it stops an inch or two short of the hole—but really, does it matter?

Now the gallery is clapping, convinced that no-one can miss a putt as easy as this one, a sentiment even I agree with. Still, to be on the safe side, I address it in a casual semblance of the standard fashion, before making the tap-in. I follow with a tiny fist pump—Tiggeresque, let's say—and look over toward Jenny. If I were on tour, this would be her cue to join me greenside for a hug and, yes, a little kiss. But I'm not on tour (not yet!) so she, Bill and I exchange the swiftest of happy hellos before I head off to attend to matters of protocol: the signing of the scorecard and such.

"So you have the best score in the foursome, I take it," a tournament official inquires.

"Guess so. A 67 today, for 135. Unofficially."

"Well then, double check it, and we'll cart you back up the 18th for the playoff," he says.

"It's a tie?"

"You and Terry Dolan."

"He shot a 66?"

"A 65. Birdied 17 and 18."

"Oh."

Suddenly there are no Oldsmobiles with which to fill my head. Instead there is only a replay of the past two holes. The chance to reach 17 eschewed in the interest of safe play. Excusable perhaps. Even prudent. But 18: Why had I not inquired what the winning score would need to be before opting to die it in? Was it due to negligence? Well, obviously—but also to hubris and overconfidence, traits a confirmed depressive should not be displaying.

Back at the 18th tee, I realize that I know Terry Dolan. He's yesterday's clubhouse skeptic, and apparently he's no less sold on either the swing or me today. "Hey, it's Stack & Tilt," he says within earshot of the gallery that follows us back. "Sixty-seven! Impressive for a four."

"Yeah, on fire today."

"Hot as a cayenne pepper," he says with a hearty laugh.

"Uh, oh, right." Only after saying this do I realize what he's referring to. Apparently he's been making inquiries. Is this guy trying to psyche me out, or does he think he's auditioning for the villain role in *Tin Cup*? It suddenly seems very important that I rise to the occasion.

In our first parry, he draws the slip of paper that will have him going first. TV commentators are sometimes heard to say that being first is an advantage because a good shot sets the bar and can even intimidate the adversary. Well, maybe—but on a hole like the 18th, where strategic considerations are so crucial, following is just fine.

Let's hope. Dolan decides to go for it, choosing much the same line as Wong but missing it right by a few yards. Likely he will be OK, in the light rough, which leaves me with no choice but to attempt the same shot as last time. Now on go the Starfire's flashers and up steps the dysfunctional yet honorable anti-hero. But something is not right with his swing. It feels like a dreaded reverse pivot and looks like it too: a low hook that dives into a lone Garry oak jutting into the left side of the fairway a good 200 yards from the hole. "Nice ball," says Dolan, somehow neglecting to add "Bwahahahahahaha."

If ever there was a tree that isn't 90 percent air, that oak is it, and I can hear my ball banging around in the branches. Sure enough, there it sits, almost stymied behind the trunk. What a loser.

I can see Dolan's ball way up ahead in what is clearly a decent lie maybe 140 from the pin. I can't count on him for anything worse than a four, so I need to punch out, then get up and down, not a comforting thought. Nothing to do about it, though, and I accomplish the first step, bounding an adept 5-iron to 155, not far from Dolan, who's now standing beside his ball, a little to the right, studying his approach while he waits. Who knows, maybe fate will be on my side.

With the Starfire parked in its stall on the green, I address the ball and make my swing. It's often said that you know where a golf ball is going just from listening. Well, there's little doubt about this one. If the terrible clanking noise doesn't give it away, the gasp of the gallery and my hastily yelled "Fore!" should help. And for those still in the dark, Dolan's anguished scream and additional scattered gasps will pretty much nail it.

CHAPTER 5
OMENS

Well, here's a test of my journalistic prowess. The other guy's still 50 feet away, so he's a little hard to hear. But I'm pretty sure the precise quotation is, "You fucking idiot. Take that swing, put it in a Porsche and burn it, you asshole. I'll stack and tilt you, you fucking loser. Fuck you. You fucking fuck."

If I've heard the last bit correctly, that's a quote from *Blue Velvet*. A cinephile!

Bill is providing play-by-play. "Just a flesh wound," he says, a moment before he reaches us. "Maybe a bad bruise." Then we see the way his wrist is already puffing up. "OK, maybe something's a little busted."

"Was that what you call a shank?" I ask.

"No," says Bill, shushing me as if the word is somehow taboo. "That was just a little snap slice."

Meanwhile, members of the gallery have gathered around the unfortunate victim, partly to attend to his injury, partly to keep him away from Jeff, who isn't precisely cowering but does appear to be on the verge of proving to be a runner, not a fighter. That's how he described himself to me—in jest, I thought at the time.

Someone with medical knowledge is attending to the wrist now. "Does that hurt?"

"Yes!" screams Dolan. "Fuuck!"

"Probably a fracture."

A couple of tournament officials are crowded around as well, inquiring whether he can go on.

"Go on? Are you kidding? He broke my wrist."

"Well, then," says one. "Tournament over. Dolan concedes the hole, which makes Jones the winner."

"Not so fast," says the other. "He has to hole out, doesn't he?"

A consultation ensues, complete with much thumbing of the rule book, apparently without definitive answer, because finally official number one agrees that, to be on the safe side, Jeff should finish the hole.

Our gallery of two dozen or so is now clustered around the officials and Dolan, who is still holding a club and looks as if he would probably swing it at Jeff if his right hand weren't so useless. The official asks Dolan once more if he is conceding, reaffirming that he can do no worse than second-place money.

"Of course I'm conceding. With only one arm I'd be lucky to get it down in 10."

Jeff's ball is in the rough, near the spot where Dolan was standing. "I wish I felt better about this," says Bill. "At least he's following his routine."

We can see Jeff staring intently at the green. Ordinarily he's conscious of the need to appear cool and laid-back, like every other guy I know. But on the golf course it all goes by the wayside, and he morphs into the byproduct of an awkward love affair between an Irish setter and a cougar destined to be shot for stalking a school child. "What's his routine?"

"Believe it or not, he visualizes a car where he wants the ball to land. An Oldsmobile."

"You're kidding, right?"

"No."

"Is that what other golfers do?"

"Yes. Some see trucks. Or boats. Ladies usually go for walk-in closets or his-and-hers bathroom vanities."

"Really?"

"No."

Jeff has finished the stare-down, and makes his swing. Once again there's the horrible noise, and the ball goes screaming off to the right, well into the trees.

He is moving very quickly now, and takes almost no time over his next shot. "He's going to chip it out. That's good," says Bill. "He still has his wits."

But an instant before the club hits the ball, Jeff makes a quick, jerky motion and the ball once again squirts right.

Jeff has a view of the green from the new spot. He pauses for a long time, making several slow and deliberate swings before stepping over the ball. "That's right," breathes Bill. "Soft and easy." But the swing is not soft and easy, and again the ball rockets right, just missing the bunkers and ending up almost against the wall of the clubhouse, where the diners and drinkers spilling out onto the patio look on with what I take to be astonishment but Bill says is closer to schadenfreude. "This is going to cost me a lot of money," he sighs.

Most of the gallery drifted away during the long delay, but others are now clustering around, and at least 40 of us follow Jeff in a tight group as he skids the ball closer and closer to the green, through flower beds and across the practice green. Finally he reaches it, and two putts later, taps the ball into the cup, to a rousing cheer.

"Easy 11," says Bill.

The presentation of trophy and check are a little, shall we say, low-key—especially as Dolan deems it necessary to stay there and glower instead of rushing off to have his wrist attended to. But I feel privileged to be part of the impromptu business meeting that follows.

"Ever had the, uh, hosel thing?" Bill asks Jeff.

"No. Hit a few on the range a couple of weeks ago, but thought I fixed it."

"OK. It's got nothing to do with Stack & Tilt, even if pros will say it does. Happens to all sorts of people all of the time. There are dozens of explanations and hundreds of cures, but none of them work."

"It can't be incurable."

"It will solve itself. Feel free to pursue any and all remedies, but in the meantime, here's what you do. Go to the drugstore and buy yourself a sling. Your story is, right after the tournament you were horsing around kicking a soccer ball and you fell down and separated your shoulder."

"I did?"

"Yes. Four weeks until the sling comes off."

"How do I teach?"

"Lots of pros teach without demonstrating. You're getting good at this; you'll just have to adapt."

"What about fixing my swing?"

"Go to the range only after the gates are locked and the lights are out. Turn some of them back on. Just make sure no-one's around."

"Because hitting hosel rockets would be bad for business."

"Very bad. Swinging a golf club with a separated shoulder wouldn't be so good, either."

"And word will get out about that playoff hole."

"Yes. You're going to be famous. Now, I gotta run. I'll find you tomorrow at your noon-hour group lesson, and you can tell me about the soccer accident. As for you, young lady, your lips are sealed."

I mime zipped lips, and Bill departs.

"You know," I say to Jeff. "This seems very serious and all, but am I wrong or did the worst shot you've ever made just win you $8,000?"

"Why, yes," he says. "I believe it did."

~ ~ ~ ~

JEFF

It's sweet the way Jenny is taking charge of the drug store situation. Perhaps she senses that I am mildly overwhelmed by the twin shocks of achieving something genuinely significant and simultaneously losing much of what I have to live for. Or maybe she understands that I'm incompetent.

"Now, which shoulder do you want it to be?" she asks.

"The right would seem more rational," I guess.

"There's nothing rational about a soccer injury," she says, giving me the stupid look. "You're right-handed and you have a stick shift. It has to be the left. So let's go in and see what they have. If we happen to need help, just let your left arm dangle. It's extremely painful and completely useless, remember that."

We find the slings in a corner beside the prescription dispensary and are attempting to determine which one would be best when Jenny grabs my arm.

"Ow!" I say, impressed with myself for catching her out in such a transparent drill.

"That's your right arm," she says. "The good one. But duck behind that shelf. We've got trouble."

Sure enough, who is lined up at the counter but Dolan, no doubt fetching some extra-strength pain killers. "I'll distract him," she says. "When the time is right, get out of here."

With that she is over to Dolan, fussing over his wrist, telling him she was in the gallery and saw the whole drama unfold.

"Close call," she says after we escape. "No X-rays yet, but the doctor thinks there's at least a bone bruise. Probably a month or more before he can play again. But you know what? He asked me for my phone number—in case, you know, he needs a witness."

"He's going to sue me?"

"No, silly." And she turns to face me, tilting a little forward. "Are you that naive?"

"Oh, right." I say, enjoying what seems to be freely granted permission to gaze down at her splendid front, which appears to have become dangerously unbuttoned. "And you gave it to him?"

"Actually, I told him my boyfriend wouldn't like that."

"Your boyfriend?"

"Need I repeat?" The stupid look again.

"What boyfriend? Oh, but did you tell him your relationship with this boyfriend is strictly platonic?"

"Well, could it be heading in a more socratic direction now?" she asks. "What do you think?"

I struggle to come up with another question, but all I can think of is an answer. "I think we should go back to my place." Much later, I forgive her last words before going to sleep, even if they do veer perilously close to cliché territory. "You know," she says. "I like a guy who takes a lot of strokes."

~ ~ ~ ~

JEFF, JUNE 4

I am whistling when I run out to get some cream for Jenny's coffee, or so I am told by the guy in the convenience store: Amy Winehouse, apparently.

"Rehab? But dude, what's with the sling? It seems like everyone's getting hurt playing golf."

"Soccer. I was playing soccer. But what do you mean?"

"Tournament you were in yesterday—guy got hit with a ball."

"Oh, yeah?"

"Seems like I underestimated you." He holds up the front page of the sports section. "You can golf *and* you can look after yourself."

"One of these, too," I say, grabbing a paper and heading out the door.

I'm a little late getting back with the cream, and more than a little steamed. "Hey, Jenny," I say, holding out the sports section. "You're a journalist. What do you think of this?"

"Very socratic of you to ask," she says, before she realizes I'm serious.

She starts reading. "This is libelous! You're 'a high-profile but controversial figure known to other members of Dunbar Gates for his fiery temper.' You 'recently returned to playing there after a long absence necessitated by a restraining order.' You're 'teaching the suddenly popular Stack & Tilt method even though you have no professional qualifications or connection to the true Stack & Tilt innovators.' This is clearly biased. Who would have written something like this without at least talking to you?"

"Maybe someone named Angie Dolan? I'd guess she's probably his wife."

"One of them anyway."

"Right." I manage a strained grin, if only to show my appreciation for her attempt to add some levity. Gallows humor, clearly, because this is serious: Who's going to take lessons from someone revealed to be a fraud and a psychopath?

I arrive at the range to find that five of the six who signed up for group Stack & Tilt fall into that category. Four aren't newspaper readers, apparently, but they're quickly brought up to date by George, the fifth.

"Heard about the tournament on the weekend," he says. "What happened to your shoulder?"

George is an 18 handicap who better be careful because adjusting his grip ever so slightly in the wrong direction will have him missing three of four fairways instead of one in two.

"Stupid accident. I was kicking around a soccer ball with some buddies after dinner last night, and I stumbled and fell." I should have left it at that but I decide to attempt a sly allusion, making a tippling gesture and adding "Too much fun."

"Ah, a drinking man too," he says.

And that's when the revelation hits. Why have a guy like George merely missing fairways when he could be hitting hosel rockets? He won't be the first person whose game goes through a rocky phase over the course of taking lessons. And surely he will learn something about the golf swing as he struggles to deal with the affliction, and maybe I will too.

So, once I have walked them through the basics, I split them up to their separate stalls and adjust their various grips, stances and alignments to something approaching the workable norm before letting them hit some balls. One by one, I coax and adjust, fairly quickly moving them toward an approximation of my swing.

"Nice, Duncan. I like that finish."

"Solid, Tim. Is your tendency always a little right, or is your concentration on the new swing causing you to let up a little with your wrists at the bottom? That's better. Nice!"

"Ah, George. How's it coming? You're an athletic guy. Let's see if we can get those hands a little higher; that shoulder needs to be pointing toward the ground; can we get that takeaway just a little more inside? Oh, your ball is squirting right? Not to worry; tough to strike it pure when you're going through swing changes."

Poor fellow.

Bill stops by as we are finishing up and sounds appropriately surprised when I tell him about my soccer accident. "Rough luck. And just when you were playing so well. Don't know if you were aware of it, but in that field there were two guys who once had status on the Nationwide, three NCAA tournament winners and two currently on the R&A's ranking of the world's 1,000 top amateurs."

"Really?"

"Yeah. And I see that Plummer and Bennett now have half a dozen Tour players switched over."

"Wow. So fast."

"Yeah, well, I'll be in the office when you're done."

That was chilling. If Bill thought it necessary to talk things up, there must be trouble. I steer George back to a semblance of form before telling everyone I'll see them again next week. I hope.

Bill isn't in his familiar spot behind the iMac, but rather at the far wall, staring up at a canvas by Vilhelm Lundstrøm, a mid-century Dane who followed in Picasso's footsteps just a little too closely, in my estimation.

"How bad is it?"

He raises an eyebrow. No doubt he is weighing whether my question indicates straightforward pessimism or I'm unexpectedly demonstrating a sliver of judgement and even intuition. "It's baddish, but nothing we can't deal with. I've had about a dozen people try to cancel today. Signed them all to ironclad contracts, so we'll keep most of them, or their money at least. A brilliant stroke to offer a 10% discount for paying in advance, if I do say so. But we'll have to give a few refunds. Just the way it is."

"That's not so terrible."

"No. There will be more, especially when they see your sling, but like I say, we'll keep most of them. Driving range operators aren't regulated in the same way car dealers are, if you know what I mean. If anyone brings it up with you, just send them in to me and I'll handle the … negotiations."

"Right."

"Then there's Dolan. Don't know if he's shot his wad. You've never represented yourself as a pro, and the range isn't PGA-affiliated, so I can't see that he has anything on us. On the other hand he's got a girlfriend that his wife doesn't know about. Hate to get involved in that sort of thing, of course."

"Of course." It's now 20 hours since the tournament ended. I spent 10 of them frolicking in bed while Bill devoted 19 of them to taking care of business like the dude wearing too much jewelry in a blaxploitation flick.

"Our lawyer is drafting a letter for the newspaper. You can have a look before it goes out. They'll stand on journalistic principle, but the bias is pretty extreme and they'll come around to a quid pro quo of some sort when they see we're not going away—maybe a feature on Stack & Tilt. The timing will be good because by then your shoulder will be healed."

"Right."

"So it's all going to work out. But just in case, I've sent out another email blast with news of your tournament win. We'll hold these ones off till the sling is gone. Booked right up and all."

"Right."

And if the worst comes to the worst, I've got a buddy with a range over in the valley. People can't read out that way, so you could easily spend a couple of days a week at his place. Work for you?"

"You're amazing."

"Just trying to put bread on the table. Of course, there's one thing you have to do."

"Fix the hosel thing. Yeah."

"No, I don't want you worrying about that. It will fix itself. But in the meantime, you have to be a prince on the range—every duffer a wanted duffer and all that."

Good lord, did he somehow see that I'd been toying with George? Or, even more chilling, in that chess grandmaster way, had he looked six moves ahead and figured out that it would ultimately cross my mind to use a student as a hosel-rocket guinea pig? "Of course. Always."

"Good, then. You should be proud of what you did yesterday. That was a tough field. Have you figured out how to spend the eight grand?"

"I don't know. Live off it? You know how it is. The quickest way to make $8,000 playing golf is to start with $80,000." I mentally curse myself for pulling that one off the shelf.

"Well, be sure and let me know if ever you should decide to trade in that, uh, automobile. I still have some connections."

"Not the plan, but you never know."

With a nice break before the after-work crowd arrives for their lessons, I have time to head home and straighten up in case I'm lucky enough to host Jenny again this evening. But the Neon does its coughing thing, and this time the heaving is so severe I can't get it to move more than a few feet, even by riding the clutch. Finally, there is a loud backfire, and the thing simply quits. Bill is already punching buttons on his phone as he walks out toward me.

~ ~ ~ ~

One hour later I am sitting inside my new car, watching as a tow truck hooks up to the old one. "Whatever you think I should buy," I'd said to Bill, after rolling down the window of the dead Neon.

"Already on its way," Bill said. "Don't worry, you'll like it."

Bill has gotten me a 2001 9.3 SE. A Saab, needless to say. He apologizes that it wasn't a pre-GM model, but for one of those I'd have to go back to the early 1990s, and that's too old for a daily driver, even if it's a Saab.

"This at least has the hatchback," he says from the passenger seat, as I survey my new steed. "And a turbo-charged, two-litre engine good for 205 horsepower. First production car to surpass the magic hundred horsepower per litre mark, I believe. With the hatch up you can put a kitchen range in the back and still go from 0-60 in under seven seconds. Only car before or since that can do that." Bill doesn't exactly throw open the windows onto how he might be feeling, but even I can sense his heart swelling with pride.

I have a difficult time applying my vast cultural studies and visioneering capabilities to the analysis of Saabs, a vehicle I now know quite a bit about, thanks to long, involved conversations with the erstwhile dealer. Prior to the 1970s, the cars were merely quirky, even by the standards of small-volume European manufacturers, a roster that at the time included such strange and little remembered marques as DAF, NSU, Jensen, Simco, Riley and Talbot, though sadly, nothing from Denmark.

But in the 1970s the American distributor espied the inroads that German companies like BMW were making with their sporty sedans and convinced the company to put a push behind the new 900 model, with its turbo option and nifty convertible. Sure enough, a sporty yet practical vehicle of European pedigree and quirkily appealing appearance proved to be exactly what certain pioneering members of the preppie/yuppie Me Generation were in search of. For a time a Saab seemed every bit as sexy as a cable-knit sweater tied around your shoulders.

But few strange cars from Scandinavia stay on top forever, or even for much more than a decade, as it turned out. The completely new 900 that GM debuted in North America in 1993 and later morphed into my 9.3, was subject to mixed reviews. It definitely lacked something in the styling department, but it was a decent car and did find a market, just not the one enjoyed earlier. Its admirers tended more to ceramicists blessed with modest inheritances and career students who'd failed to complete their dissertations but did manage to nab that faculty position at the community college. A lot of Syd's architect friends had also proven vulnerable, for seemingly inexplicable reasons that become clearer after seeing the buildings they conceived. If you find a Volvo too stolid, a Subaru too frumpy, a Lexus too subdued, an

Infiniti too boy-racer, a Mercedes too establishment, a BMW too aspirational, an Audi too Volkswagen and a Volkswagen too Mazda, well, Saab exists to fulfill your highly stratified automotive desires. Improbably, there are just enough people of the type that the marque ultimately outlived Oldsmobile, an eventuality that filled Bill with a kind of wonder.

And now I have a European near-luxury sport sedan of my own, even if it's the weird one and six years old. Naturally I gun it a couple of times on the way to and back from the apartment. It's definitely no Neon, nor even a Mazda 6, my last lease, chosen after easily rejecting the bland-beyond-belief Camcords and what not that my position at the company granted me.

In light of what happened to a certain colleague's Porsche Cayenne, I've carefully examined myself for symptoms of auto envy: Could my irritation with Kevin have been partly explained by his unexpected and unwarranted promotion to a VP position and subsequent acquisition of a vehicle carefully calculated to emphasize his success and virility? Alternatively, was the irritation partly due to Syd's apparent vulnerability to the kind of man who would advertise his success so blatantly?

These were reasonable conjectures, I ultimately concluded, but unsupported by the facts. No, I was irritated with Syd and Kevin because, behind my back and out of nowhere, they conspired to get naked together.

But none of that is important anymore because I have moved on. My inkling is that Bill's right about not sweating the hosel thing. Experience suggests that small flaws need to be worked on, while career-threatening, life-ruining, massively debilitating ones are best ignored. Well, it doesn't suggest that, actually, but what can I do? Before I beat myself up on the range at two in the morning, I'll do some research, maybe even talk with someone like Matt. In the meantime recent events and my light Monday schedule conspire to make personal matters more important than golf ones, and how long has it been since I've been in a position to say that? On the brand new cell phone I picked up this morning, I punch the single number I've so far managed to store, it of the very frisky, funny, smart, sweet and—did I mention frisky?—Jenny.

"Hello, Jeff?"

"None other."

"A cell phone!"

"You're my first call."

"Your first! I'm so flattered. And excited."

"Still?"

"Still."

"You're a surprisingly excitable person."

"You're making me blush."

"Maybe I'm being too bold, but I'm done at the range and all I can think about is how much I'd like to be with you. If you can stand the excitement."

"Oh yeah, the excitement's fine. Let me rephrase that: I'm getting excited just thinking about the excitement. But I have a little hitch on the home front. You know that I was complaining about my stove. Well, the building manager says there's no money for upgrades but I can go ahead and fix up anything if I want to pay for it myself."

"Yeah."

"Anyway, so I was looking on Craigslist."

"Strictly Furniture or Casual Household Goods?" Aware of Bill's Craigslist strategy and my clumsy attempt to emulate it, Jenny laughs at this.

"Anyway, I bought a stove."

"You bought a stove?"

"Yeah, and it has to be picked up this evening, period. But all the delivery companies are booked up, so I'm working the phone trying to find a way to get it over here."

"Sweetie?"

"Yeah?"

"How fast did you say you needed that stove delivered?"

~ ~ ~ ~

JEFF, JUNE 5

"Oh, hi Mom."

"Hiroshi! How come you didn't return my messages?"

"Sorry. I was playing all weekend in a tournament."

"The golf?"

"Aye."

"You should get a cell phone."

"Maybe some day."

"How was the golf?"

"It was good. Mostly good. Well, I won the tournament."

"That's wonderful. Was it a real tournament?"

"Huh? Yes, it was real."

"I mean, a big tournament?"

"Pretty big. All the local pros. Lots of top amateurs. I won $8,000."

"Wonderful! That's a lot of money for you. So you're a good golfer."

"You could say that."

"It all makes so much sense."

"What do you mean?"

"Your athletic ability. Your dad being a baseball player. You know."

"Sure I have some athletic ability. But I've hit 250,000 range balls in the past year. Probably more than Vijay Singh."

"Pardon?"

"Practice. I've had a lot of practice."

"Anyone can practice. But not everyone wins. Plus you have the heterosis advantage. To think that they laughed at me."

"They laughed for a good reason."

"See, you laugh."

"Yes, I laugh."

"You've heard of the Flynn Effect, maybe?"

"Maybe not."

"Average IQs have risen 20 points since the tests first came out. It's called the Flynn Effect. And no-one could explain it."

"Because the tests are culturally specific and people have figured them out."

"That's what someone who wasted his time at university might say, someone who doesn't know anything about science. Actually, you people would like the Flynn Effect because the most stupid people are rising the fastest and that would seem a good thing to you."

"Stupid people getting less stupid would be a good thing. So tell me, why are IQs rising?"

"Well, heterosis for one thing."

"Is that your latest theory?"

"Not mine. Michael Mingroni at the University of Delaware wrote the first paper. Everybody's talking about it."

"Oh, come on. We mulattos are only about five percent of the population. There aren't enough of us to skew the numbers."

"OK, it's not so much the races. The whole race idea is misleading, I'll give you that. There are genetic distinctions between human populations, but they don't conform that well to, you know, Negro, Caucasian, Asian."

"Glad to hear you say that."

"Science says that. But when you mix people from all over the place in big cities and they start to mate—bingo, heterosis! It isn't the only reason for increased IQs, but it's one of them. Maybe for increasing heights, too."

"And this is for real?"

"Yes, it's for real. Peer review. The whole enchilada. Just like I always said. Except, I didn't know about it not being the races and also, well, I didn't realize you would be such a good example: a championship golfer and quite smart too."

"Now you think I'm smart?"

"Yes, and maybe you're getting smarter. A lot smarter than you were a year ago, I think."

"Thanks for the memories. And to what do I owe the pleasure of this conversation?"

"Be nice to your mother. I just wanted to update you on the preparations."

"OK. So, what's new?"

"Well, I heard back from your father. He's very excited. You were going to make some recommendations about where to go? I haven't been back in two years."

"Yeah, I talked to Bill, my business partner. I told you he's pretty up on this stuff. He wondered if it would be appropriate to riff on our, uh, ethnic heritage. There's a new kind of Japanese place called an izakaya: not sushi; dozens of strange dishes and a lot of fun."

"In Japan an izakaya is more of a pub, but sure, maybe."

"And another place that's central American—more Guatemalan than Nicaraguan, but who knows what the difference would be?"

"The man doesn't want to fly all this way to eat crappy food from back home."

"Then how about the intensely local thing? Local seafood, animals from the farm, vegetables from the plot out back? You've heard the word locavore, right?"

"Locavore? Sounds strange, but new is good, I suppose. Where is this place, in the country?"

"There are three or four, maybe more. A couple downtown, another just off campus, another …"

"Let's do the campus one. I spent 35 years there. You were there for a long, long time. We could go for a walk afterwards. It's light until 9:30. I like that. Will you make the reservation?"

"OK, for Friday?"

"Sure. That's the night I get to meet your new girlfriend."

"Jenny."

"Yes, Jenny. I hope she's nice."

"Yeah, thanks for that. And Saturday at the izakaya?"

"Sure. Syd is coming?"

"That's the plan."

"What will your girlfriend think?"

"She's fine. I've already told her."

"She won't want to come?"

"She didn't say anything."

"Of course she didn't. But she'll be suspicious and hurt."

"No. Really? I could ask her."

"You should. Syd's great, but she and you are over. Think of the future. You're a smart boy now."

"Right, as always, Mom. Is that all?"

"That's all."

"Bye, then."

"Love you, Hiroshi."

~ ~ ~ ~

JEFF, JUNE 26

"So what do you think, Dr. Bill? Is there any law saying a guy can't swing a golf club again after only 23 days?"

"Well, yours seems to have been a fairly mild case, perhaps only Type 1 rather than the Type 2 I originally diagnosed. At least based on all the late-night success I've been hearing about. On the range, I mean."

It's a relief to hear a double entendre from Bill, given all the single entendres he's been lobbing my way. The next time I feel a need to chip in with the male bonding, I'll talk baseball, and not a word about women who are proving to be even more fun than they look.

"Yes, my hosel hasn't had any action in days."

There's a beat as Bill tries to think of a ribald response, but apparently nothing comes to mind. "OK, but tell me you're not thinking of entering the big tournament on the weekend."

"I was thinking about it. Gas is going through the roof, and this damn Saab takes premium, you know."

"OK, here's the deal. It's hard to see an upside. If you do badly you'll become an object of ridicule—the shank guy. Do well, and you'll become a target. The shank and tilt guy."

"Nice coinage. "

"No offence. That's just what people will say."

"But I'm not just Jeff, the Stack & Tilt teacher. I'm also Jeff, the guy who loves to golf and who's getting pretty good at it. You said it yourself: I beat three guys who have won NCAA tournaments. Two guys in the Royal & Ancient's Top 1,000."

"Yes, and next time they'll beat you. That's golf."

"But the point is, I'm in the game. I belong out there with those guys."

"True. You're a Saab, though. Sometimes all the weird bits get put together just right and the Saab beats the BMW. But in between, it's just one damn thing after another. Oh man, why couldn't I have gone with a Toyota for once?"

"You'd rather have a Toyota than me? What, a taupe Corolla?"

"No, no."

"A Tauporolla? For people who want their automotive appliance to coordinate with the decor?"

"Jeez, sorry Jeff. I know how that must sound."

"Maybe an Echo?

"Oh, come on."

"With a trunk instead of a hatch because Americans don't like hatches? Or an Avalon? For people who still can't get over not being able to buy an Oldsmobile?"

Bill is squirming. I'm completely incompetent at trash talk, but apparently a talented practitioner of its passive-aggressive cousin: getting at the other guy by dissing yourself.

"Oh, man. I owe you an apology. That came out wrong. You know how much I love Saabs."

"Have you been working too hard?"

"Actually, I think I have." In his entire life Bill has probably never been asked the question.

"Too much cleaning up behind me?"

"Well, there has been a bit of, uh, negotiating. But no, it's just everything. Trying to get the expansion happening, finding a way to pay for it."

"Stock market's up. Credit's cheap. Bernanke's in for Greenspan, and the Goldilocks economy rolls right along."

"Yeah, but there's something weird going on out there. Don't know quite what."

"How could you even tell? I read in the paper that Moodys and Standard and Poors just downgraded a bunch of subprime bonds. I don't even know what subprime bonds are."

"That's when you buy crap mortgages, I think. But, like you say, who knows what's going on? Sometimes it's important, sometimes it isn't, and there's no way for people like us to tell. I just know that there's something strange with the business. Range revenues are down 4% this year."

"Me not paying for my balls—there's your problem right there."

"Yeah, mystery solved. But it's the same at other places. The courses. The equipment stores."

"Maybe the rain."

"Checked that. The year's been pretty normal."

"Just a blip, probably. But now that you mention it, did you notice how slow things are going at Garry Oaks?"

"Apparently just 15,000 rounds played there last year."

"Well, it was supposed to be private, but they couldn't sell the real estate. I asked the guy: He didn't want to admit it, but only 20 lots in two years."

"Nice place. Why would that be?"

"It seems like it's happening at other developments too."

"What, real estate not selling?"

"Yeah. Prices dropping in a few places. Sometimes quite a lot."

"That is weird. What do you think?" Bill has a puzzled look on his face, which is unusual.

"Ever hear of Ivy Zelman—Poison Ivy?"

"Nope."

"She's a stock analyst who covers the real estate sector. Thinks there's a massive oversupply of housing."

"Well, duh."

"Yeah, basically that the whole thing is going to come crashing down."

"Holy shit, wouldn't that change things in a hurry. You don't follow the stock market?"

"Not in the slightest."

"So you've never heard of the Hindenburg Omen."

"Never."

"Well, it's a technical indicator—the kind of thing that guys with green visors look for. Happens when a bunch of stocks hit new lows and a bunch of other ones hit new highs. They think it's unnatural."

"Like Stack & Tilt—or homosexuality."

I wonder how Bill will respond to my stupid remark. His natural car dealer instincts make him something of a libertarian even if, crypto-Scandinavian that he is, he sometimes muses about the wonders of social democracy. Sadly lacking in the eight years I spent hanging around campus on my way to six years' worth of degrees, the self-made man admits that he finds himself poorly armed to consider matters of an ideological nature. Still and whatever, he's as liberal as it gets on social matters. His only complaint with gays would be that they don't spend a lot of money at the driving range. Well, the guys, anyway.

Bill appears not to even notice my slight, if that's what it was. He's a white guy who's spent a lifetime overhearing slurs and jibes and barely even notices them, lucky fellow. "I don't know if I've mentioned it, but I play a little on the markets myself," he says. "You know about the Japanese carry trade, I imagine."

"Uh, not really. I can't say I've fully explored the Japanese side of my lineage."

"Nothing to do with that. Just a side effect of the big property bust back in the early '90s. Because there's been essentially no growth there, interest rates are close to zero."

I have no idea what this could mean to an investor and might as well admit it. "Uh?"

"So investors can borrow money in Japan at pretty much no cost and plow it into the markets somewhere else, or buy bonds at a higher interest rate, or invest in something else. As long as the yen doesn't go down, it's a sure thing."

Of course. So simple. "And you do that?"

"My broker has access to an investment pool, and I buy in on a small scale. But last week I started dialing back on the leverage."

"Why?"

"Well, among other things, the Hindenburg Omen."

"You base your investing strategy on an omen?"

"It isn't exactly reading the entrails. Every major sell-off since the '80s has been preceded by an occurrence, and in the past two weeks there have been three of the damn things."

"Well, whatever. I don't believe in omens."

"Why not?"

"Believing in omens assumes the ability to recognize them, and I'm completely lacking in insight or intuition."

"Hey, is that your phone?"

It is my phone, for which I have yet to develop the standard Pavlovian response. "Hi, Jenny."

"Hi, Sport. What are you up to?"

"Just talking with Dr. Bill. He says my sling can come off."

"That's great. Now you can take me golfing. Finally."

"Absolutely."

"Soon too, because I'm going to be away all weekend."

"Where?"

"L.A. I fly out early on Friday. A magazine thing."

"That's great. I guess."

"I'd invite you, but I'm going to hook up with an old college pal."

"Hook up?"

"Not that way! She's an old roommate. Nothing exciting in the least."

"OK, glad to hear it. It will have to be tomorrow, then. 2 o'clock?

"Perfect."

"I'll pick you up."

"Thanks, Jeff."

"That settles that. Jenny's away on the weekend, so I'm playing golf."

"We'll both be thinking of you and your hosel."

"Right, Bill."

~ ~ ~ ~

JEFF, JUNE 27

In a perfect golf world, there would be more executive-length courses with decent greens, a nifty hole or two and $25 green fees. That way more people could afford the time and money, and hackers and beginners wouldn't need to feel useless and worthless because their five-hour rounds wreck it for everyone else on the big courses. Conversely, those of us from the big courses could show up every now and then for a little R&R.

Building more courses like that might even make financial sense because, damn, this place is busy. On a Wednesday afternoon in June, you'd expect to cruise around in under three hours with the helmets off, because only a few other people would be hooking and slicing at you from adjacent fairways. Instead, we wait 30 minutes to get out, and even then we're grouped with another twosome, the ominously named Adam and Yves.

Jenny is taken with the agricultural theme, which is achieved via a barn-like clubhouse and antique tractors parked around at various spots. She suggests the course must be owned by Bill's rural alter ego—a one-time Minneapolis-Moline dealer outraged that those ugly green John Deeres triumphed over his superior line despite their failure to adopt three-point hitches in a timely manner.

"What's a three-point hitch?"

"The industry-standard coupling between tractors and the equipment they pull, widely adopted in the 1960s. Anyone who's written for *Western Tractor* would know that," Jenny says.

"Sorry for even having to ask."

"My favorite Minnie ever was the U-DLX Comfortractor. Imagine it's 1938, and farmers are starting to make some money again. The horses are being put out to pasture, but do you spring for both a tractor and a truck or spend the money on a really nice tractor, complete with a cab, a heater and a radio, plus an extra seat for the missus?"

"The latter, I guess."

My response garners the stupid look. "I forget. You're a Saab man. A tractor with leather upholstery and streamlined styling would make perfect sense to you."

"I hope the key is on the floor. Does it come in black? Sunroof? Heated seats? Hey, maybe we'll see one on the course."

"Not likely. Only 150 of them sold and maybe a dozen or two remain in existence. They go for six figures these days. It would be like finding a Duesenberg in a barn."

Well, then. For perhaps the first time, I find myself anticipating the decoration of the course as much as the design, which in the tradition of such places manages to be prosaic yet weird. The name, though, kind of rocks—no doubt a reference to the provenance of the site, an old farm that's been preserved in places with rows of mature fruit trees separating the fairways. That makes for too many straight lines, but there are a few design aspects that work, and someone even seems to have had a sense of humor. Jenny's knowledge of tractors doesn't measure up to Bill's of cars, but she is able to identify the ancient model sitting behind the first green as a John Deere D, which had only two cylinders and so was known by farmers as a putt-putt.

Adam and Yves, on the other hand, appear to be relics from another aspect of our proud heritage, the industrial one. Although still in their twenties, the two each had a decade of work behind them at a window manufacturer when they were laid off a few weeks ago. I'm familiar with the company and its excellent fir and hemlock windows and doors, so news of its troubles comes as a bit of a shock.

"But those are some of the best windows in the business. We specified them on our high-end condos."

"You betcha," says Adam, who, halfway down the first fairway, has already opened one of the beers from the six-pack he's carting along. "Right on," adds Yves, who is into his own six-pack.

"So, what happened?"

"Not really sure. Two months ago everything was booming, and then orders just dried up. We expect to get called back in soon, but until then, dude, let's golf!"

Their enthusiasm is admirable even if their golf games aren't. Adam is stooped, loose and handsy, but at least most of his parts are in the right place. Earlier, watching him take a couple of warm-up swings, I guessed he might break 100 on the par-61 course. It's Yves who will have trouble beating even Jenny, who has never golfed before but has a month of instruction under her belt and won't make a lot of really bad shots.

Optimism nonetheless prevails as we reach our widely distributed tee shots. Jenny's near the middle of the fairway, 130 yards from the pin on the short par-4. From there she makes another good swing, pushing the ball just right of the small green. With his sloppy outside-in swing, Adam managed to keep his banana of a tee shot on the right edge of the fairway 80 yards from the green. Now he scuttles his second into a bunker that guards it.

Yves lined up for his drive with his hands slightly separated and in front of the ball by at least a foot. From that unnatural position he somehow managed a three-quarter swing, muscling a line shot that pierced the trees arrayed along the left side, penetrating well onto the next fairway. Now he manages to get back onto our side, though not before bouncing off a couple of boughs. Both Adam and Yves require four shots to reach the green, where finally we get to my ball, which I'd plopped down onto the left edge, after bending in a 275-yard fade.

And so it goes for several holes: Jenny misdirecting lots of questions about the game but sticking her ball to the fairway while chalking up steady bogies and doubles; Adam and Yves chunking and flailing; me alternating between pars and birdies with a rare eagle thrown in, even if it's on an admittedly dubious 260-yard par-4. There are also some pretty cool tractors—including, points out Jenny, a massive steam engine from the teens, when farmers pulled their plows and powered their threshing machines using coal.

Finally, on the 14th, Yves asks for help. It can't have escaped his notice that Jenny has never golfed before, yet is beating the two of them by several strokes, while I am about to set a course record, if such a thing exists.

"Are you some kind of pro?" Yves asks.

"Not a PGA pro, but yeah, I do teach. Ever heard of Stack & Tilt?"

"No."

"Well, it's a new kind of swing. It looks pretty standard to most people, but there are some significant differences. Getting a lot of publicity right now because quite a few touring pros are switching over."

In the hierarchy of tired clichés, "eyes lighting up" is right at the top, but, that said, Yves eyes' light up. Even a person as perceptive as me can read the thought balloon above his head. With his ultra-strange swing, he has doubtless received lots of critiques and advice. But he doesn't like being helped, doesn't want to be one of those golf robots and, in any case, manages to blast out a good shot often enough to give himself hope. Sure, he could take lessons, but wouldn't it be better to perfect his own swing and school his ass-hat buddies?

But the more he golfs, the more he realizes that just isn't going to happen, and now here I am, offering the prospect of an obviously workable swing that's different from the one his friends advise. Also, he's on his fifth beer and the two have shared a couple of reefers. "Hey, coach," Yves says. "Don't suppose you have any pointers for me."

On the 15th tee there is plenty of time to kill, thanks to the geriatrics ahead of us, so I subject Adam and Yves to the most perfunctory of diagnostics: Grip, stance, alignment. I explain the principles behind Stack & Tilt, and insist they keep their left heels on the ground, but there is otherwise little about the swing I have them attempting that they wouldn't learn from another pro. Still, it pleases them that what they are doing is at least a little unconventional—and so colorfully named. "Am I stacked?" asks Adam. "You're on tilt," replies Yves. I pretend not to notice the second part of the response. "She's stacked."

Jenny is indeed stacked, but she's also stoked. On the par-4 18th, a pond complete with fountain just short and right of the green has her needing a fade instead of the consistent draw she's been showing all day, a function of her tidy inside-out swing. Golf virgin though she is, Jenny nevertheless recognizes this, and asks me what she can do. There are a dozen different ways to set yourself up for a fade, of course, but I suggest just two, a slightly more open stance and a takeaway that's a little more outside, which I have her rehearse several times before making a swing. Somewhat astonishingly, she fades her 5-wood onto the fringe, then gets up and down for her second par of the day.

With their new swings Adam and Yves also net pars to go with my birdie, leaving us a happy bunch as we head for the 19th. "You know what would really make my day," says Jenny, as we shake hands. "One of those peaches."

Sure enough, the tree she's spotted behind the green has a nice crop of fruit, so we wander over to see what can be plucked. It appears we're not the first to find them, however, and there is nothing to be reached from ground level. "Yeah, I sure could eat a peach," says the always witty Yves, which seems to inspire Adam. "Least we can do is get the Stack & Tilt babe a peach," he says.

And with that he is clambering up the spindly shrub, aiming for the fruits that dangle 10 or 12 feet above. For a big, drunk guy, he manages to get himself onto a crotch about seven feet up with surprising ease. Unfortunately, his weight is too much and one of the branches breaks, destroying half the tree and sending him tumbling onto the ground.

It takes Adam five or 10 seconds to get to his knees, and when he does he is holding his shoulder and groaning. "What is it, dude?" says Yves, who hovers over his buddy.

"Gawd, my shoulder."

Yves, who says he has his first aid ticket, gently manipulates Adam's arm, as the woman we paid our green fees to arrives on the scene.

"Who did this to the tree?" she's shouting. "You. Were you climbing it? That tree was 50 years old. You guys are out of here. Blacklisted," she says. "Don't ever come back."

Yves continues the examination. "Dude," he says. "That's a shoulder separation."

Jenny glances over in astonishment. "Guess the pros were wrong," she says. Stack & Tilt doesn't cause cancer. Just separated shoulders."

"Man, rough luck," I say. "Bright side? I happen to have a sling in the car."

~ ~ ~ ~

SYD, JUNE 28

So Jeff wants to get together for lunch. Weird message, even for him. Wants to talk about something. Heavy.

I wish I were more certain that nothing could be stupider than getting back with him. The trouble is, he's a fescue, and there aren't many fescues around, sad to say. Lots of bents and blue grasses, but who wants those if you can have a fescue? Hardy and low-maintenance. Looks beautiful to a seasoned eye, and plays the absolute best. Fescue's the ideal turf grass in every way, except maybe that it doesn't stand up to traffic. That's Jeff. If he were a golf course I'd limit him to 20,000 rounds a year. Make sure he gets lots of recovery time.

But he's in terrific shape right now, I'm told. You'd think that newspaper article would have tipped him back over the edge. Now, that was a trampling and a half. But Dad says he's doing great. Separated his shoulder too, and it hardly seemed to bother him.

Apparently he's been dating someone. Well, that would have made calling me up for lunch even harder. Courageous! But what does it all mean?

I only wish I weren't so horny. For the first time in my life I understand why some people don't just talk and joke about sex, they obsess over it. Because they're not having it, of course. Or they're my mom. Or these days, they're me. What happened to all that resolve about sex with the ex? But enough. Let's get the mind out of the gutter, compose one's super-confident self, and walk through this door.

"Jeff!"

"Syd. You look great!"

"Likewise. Of course everyone looks good in here. Lolita, Jeff? Since when are you the guy who lunches at the trendy restaurant that everyone who's anyone is talking about?"

"Since I became a suave man-about-town."

"And you are a suave man-about-town, I hear."

Before he can respond, we are interrupted by the waiter, who wonders what we would like to drink. Jeff jumps right in, hoping that I don't mind sharing a bottle of the terrific little Grüner-Veltliner he's spotted on the list. "Fine, then," he twinkles, after confirming that it's the 2005. "We'd like that shaken, not stirred."

Something seems to have happened to the man I used to know, and I don't hate it. Flutter.

Now he is asking me about work. Is that the appropriate thing to do? Yes, I'm going to give him this one. It's true that we are exes who know each other intimately and recently shared a moment of sorts. But we haven't spoken for weeks, and we both know that something has to be broached, while only one of us knows what it is. Under the circumstances, work is a good way in.

"Oh, you know, that stupid mortgage company headquarters I told you about. They've been a total pain, and now it looks like the thing is being put on hold. How a mortgage company could have money troubles isn't clear, but that's what they're saying. What, they can't get a mortgage? But it's a bummer, because there isn't a lot of work in the pipeline."

"That's what Bill at the range was saying." This leads to a discussion of the economy and how it's so weird right now, a perfectly reasonable conversation for two people who have businesses to run, except for its extended duration. Long after the food arrives, we are still talking about, no shit, the Japanese carry trade.

"So," I finally say. "I hear you've been seeing someone." Bringing this up was never my intention, but we've had two and a half glasses of wine, and we're a man and a woman talking about something called the Hindenburg Omen?

"Well, yes," says Jeff. "Jenny. But she's out of town for a few days."

Well, that was predictable. Now what? Is this our cue to order another glass of wine, leading to a furtive drive home to my place?

"So the cat's away," I say without any suggestion of lasciviousness. There's no hint whatsoever that what I'm thinking is "So the pussy's away, hey, big boy." No hint. Of course, Jeff is familiar with the workings of a London mind, and my intentions are probably transparent. But dammit, this is his gig. He better take the lead here.

"Uh, so, I was talking to my mom, and she was worried that Jenny might be hurt if there were another woman at the restaurant with my dad. Especially my, uh, ex-wife. You."

"Your mom was worried?"

"Yes, quite worried."

"And what do you think?"

"Well, that's the thing that I wanted to talk to you about."

So he's invited me to a drunken lunch at a fancy place to disinvite me from dinner with his father? Well, fair enough. Yeah, I'm crushed, but he's got a new girlfriend that he seems to like a lot and, you know, I think his mom is probably right. Except that he can't seem to spit it out himself, so it's up to me, the victim, to do all the work.

"OK, no problem, message received," I say. "I have to run. Thanks for lunch."

Ever the sport I get up and walk out the door. Back in the day I would have said what needed to be said, but then he probably knows it anyway: Yeah, dude, that was the fescue thing to do, but it sure wasn't the fescue way to do it.

CHAPTER 6
WHAT KIND OF SCIENCE

JEFF, JUNE 29, 2007

Syd once told me that other people tend to see her dad as a dashing Sean Connery or Robert Redford, but he's actually more of a hard-ass whose true film alter-ego is closer to Clint Eastwood. Well, I've never seen any sign of the psychic scars that make Eastwood such a compelling hero, but I will allow that Sam seems to be awfully good at getting what he wants, no matter how he has to do it. His cap is back down to 2, and he's not ready to concede the club championship to anyone, he tells me during our weekly lesson. He won it at 46 and again at 56. A lot of people thought that was pretty cool, but 66—well, with three weeks to go, no-one better be writing him off.

We're at 11:30 this week, so that we can have something to eat afterward. Which might be a mistake. Recent sit-downs with Londons have not gone really well, and it's not as if I'm the kind of person who should be lunching two days in a row, in any case. Still, an hour of forced intimacy with Sam can't be so bad. He's a good guy, of course. More than that, business really seems to intrigue me these days, and there's the prospect of catching up with his entrepreneurial efforts. Bill has tipped me to a little bistro-style place not far from the range, and as we are arranging ourselves at the table I attempt to shift into neo-Jeff mode and ask him what's new.

"Well, I'm working on something with Georgia. Something genuinely creative that we've come up with all by ourselves."

"Another installation? Time lapse again? Mud cracking this time, Sam?" I hope I am doing well in my endeavor to be an engaging conversationalist.

"Nope. None of that fine art stuff. A retail concept."

"Really?"

"Yes. It came out of her board work. Lots of donors and visiting VIPs that have to be given thank yous and such. The gifts really should be something local, but how much time can you put into tracking down the perfect artifact? Shouldn't there be a shop that does it for you?"

"I guess."

"You're familiar with the locavore thing?"

"Sure." Of course I'm familiar with one of the keystone concepts of the 21st century, and have been for days.

"Well, we're calling this LocaStore."

"Catchy." If Sam has a weakness as a human being, it's his tendency to get just a little too enthusiastic about the wares he is selling—to believe his own bullshit, as people at the company were fond of saying way too often. Back there the trait was considered part of a good salesman's toolkit, at least to a point. No doubt it has contributed to Sam's considerable success, but really.

"You're skeptical. Because you're a man and getting and giving gifts isn't important to you. And you're more of a rationalist like me who doesn't place a lot of value in souvenirs and keepsakes. But we're in the minority, and some day even you will be looking for the perfect thing to give someone or fill a spot on the wall—a totem pole pennant from the 1950s or an original, framed 19th-century explorer's map—and you won't know where to look. You'll try eBay, but if you don't happen to find exactly what you're looking for, it won't point you to something that's even better. And then you'll realize that there's a store that sells everything from here that a person could ever want."

"Like a baseball program with my dad's name on the lineup."

"Not sure we can find one of those for you. If not, there will be something else. Maybe a drink coaster from the bar the players used to hang out at."

I hadn't realized that Sam was familiar with the opening minutes of my life story, but obviously Syd must have said something. Life would be more pleasant if fewer people knew about my provenance as a human fruit fly.

"And the next time you're in that position you'll know that this is the place to go for something different. Signed first editions by local authors. Movie flyers from the grand old cinema that got torn down. Colorized postcards of old motels. Rock festival posters from the Sixties. We've been garage-saling for a couple of years and we have a storage locker full of the stuff. But maybe two-thirds of the merchandise will be new. Original art, clothes, design items and artisanal stuff by local names. Plus cool crap that's made in China and sells for five bucks: pins, decals, spoons, coffee mugs—pens where some poor thing loses her bikini."

"That's local?"

"You've never been to our fabulous nude beach?"

"Actually, no."

"Really. I would have thought that Syd … ah well, generation gap."

"So will this poor thing have pubic hair?" I don't know why I would ask such a thing, but we are two men carrying several millennia worth of cultural baggage and a fascination with the pudendum that transcends eras, continents, cultures and religions. Plus the topic has received extensive media coverage in recent years and, in any case, seems to come up regularly in my dealings with the London family.

Sam passes if off as standard man talk. "She will if Georgia does the ordering. She's a proponent of a back to the bush movement." He smiles. "Her next great cause."

This marks yet another thing over which mother and daughter will be at odds, but I decline to mention this. Sam wouldn't have any knowledge of Syd's new coif, and, for that matter, I'm not supposed to either.

"Also, food and wine. You know about the 100-Mile Diet, right?"

"Of course." Thanks to Bill matters of a gustatory nature are a fixation of the middle-aged and affluent with which I am no longer embarrassingly unfamiliar.

"Well, we've been on it for years. Georgia gets in her Prius and drives a hundred miles every Saturday going to this shop, and that market, and the farm where a certain cheese is made. So now people like her will be able to switch to the five-mile version and get a lot of that stuff at one spot."

"OK, cool enough. But is there a business in it?"

"Here in town, that's hard to predict. It probably makes sense more as a pilot project. Seattle would be a better bet, or up in Vancouver with the Olympics coming. Or imagine New York or San Francisco. We can launch it here because we know what we should stock and where to find it. If it works we'll just keep expanding. Franchise the concept to people who can curate their own local stores. Figure out the web side. The economy's great, and the banks are practically begging me to borrow money."

"You're not worried about the Hindenburg Omen?"

"What's that?"

"I'm not sure. Some technical stock thing that has Bill spooked. He's easing up on the markets right now. Thinks there's something weird going on."

"Really? I've never been a big equities guy. The market's scorching hot, I know, but I just don't trust it. My own stuff is pretty risky, so I try to balance that with safe investments. You're familiar with the Stanford Financial Group, probably."

"To be completely clear, I haven't been in a position to invest a lot of money lately."

Sam smiles in acknowledgement of my acknowledgement of my straightened financial circumstances. "The Stanford St. Jude Championship on Tour? Woody Austin won it last weekend."

"Sure."

"Well, it's a bank in the Caribbean."

"Tax dodge."

"No. Well, sure, maybe some people use it that way. I just like that I can get a double digit-return without any risk."

"You get 10% on, like, a bank deposit?"

"Actually, a bit higher than that."

"That's amazing. You don't find that suspicious?"

"Not really. If you look around there are quite a few investments with double-digit yields. Commercial real estate trusts get around that, some dividend stocks, hedge funds. But again, those carry a bit of risk. I have a buddy who gets more than 10% year after year from an investment fund in New York. The guy who runs it used to be chairman of the National Association of Securities Dealers, and it couldn't be safer, he says. And there are always mortgage-backed securities, of course. Who's going to default on a mortgage if it means losing your house?"

"I suppose, when you put it that way." That's Sam, ever the sensible one, bringing things back to fundamentals and first principles. "So why wouldn't you use the Japanese carry trade, and play with more?"

"Leverage? Like I say, I'm leery of risk, but I guess that makes me pretty much the last one left. Half the guys in the club quit work at 50 and just flip houses or find some hedge fund or other financial thing with double-digit returns. Not hard to do if you've got half a million equity in your house. Find some deal that gives you a line of credit at five percent and invest it in something that pays out 20. Almost a six-figure income right there."

"No wonder you're the only one foraging through last century's patent filings."

"Yeah, realistically, it's not the time to embark on risky retail ventures either. I'm a pensioner now, you know: time to grow up. But all I really like to do is cook up schemes. And play golf."

"And you're so good at both of those things."

"Right, and what's new with you?"

I know little of the ways of humans, but one thing I have observed is that dishing someone a compliment will usually result in a change of subject. Most people prefer to be the object of conversation, but are aware that, sadly, other people too wish to talk about themselves and an accommodation must be made. A compliment has the effect of sparking that realization. So, true to the conventions of his species, Sam must now train the conversation on me. He knows that I don't crave the spotlight and rarely have anything very interesting to say, so I'm unlikely to dominate for long.

"Well, I'm gonna play in another big tournament this weekend."

"Is that the one at Fenwick?"

"Yeah."

"Ever played that course?"

"Just once, maybe eight years ago,"

"Tricky, old-school layout, right? A lot of fun, and not as easy as it looks."

"That's how I remember it."

"I've played it a couple dozen times. Dunbar has reciprocal privileges, and I got to know some of the guys there."

"Tips welcome."

"Here's one, then: You should have a caddy."

"That probably would have been a good idea, but I've left it kind of late."

"Yeah, well, your caddy should be me."

"Really?"

At that moment our glasses of wine arrive, except that there has clearly been a mistake. Instead of the nice rosé that Sam ordered and I seconded, these are both red. "Out of the rosé?" Sam asks.

"Rosé?" replies the young woman. "But didn't you say "White Rose?"

"No, 'Nice rosé.'"

"No problem; I'll go get them," says the server.

"Wait," says Sam. "So this is the White Rose whole-cluster Burgundian-style pinot noir, the one that runs maybe 40 bucks a bottle at the winery?"

"That's the one," she says, cottoning on to Sam's intent. "Would you like these instead? I'll just charge you for the rosé."

"Looks like this is going to be someone's lucky weekend," I say.

"Let's drink to it."

~ ~ ~ ~

JUNE 30

When I pick Sam up at 7, Georgia is at the door in her housecoat. Oddly, as much as I've been seeing Sam, it's been 13 months for her, and I get a big hug. I never understood Syd's difficulties with her mom, her mom not being my mom. "Play well," Georgia says as we leave, one of many golfisms that she's picked up despite never having swung a club.

When Sam asks me how intrusive I'd like my caddy to be, I respond that I trust him to tell me anything he thinks I need to know, and that I'll especially be leaning on him for advice around the greens. I seem to recall that they are very undulating, and prone to breaking in all sorts of directions.

"Yeah, it's an A.V. Macan course," says Sam. "You can't have too much local knowledge."

"That's a name that keeps popping up. I should be more familiar."

"Well, he's rumoured to have done the original routing at Dunbar Gates, and maybe the greens and bunkering too. Odd situation, as maybe you know. The course was built by a private developer and both he the original club went bust from the Depression before they could even get the place open. Our club was formed to buy it from the bank. The developer disappeared, and no-one thought to ask Macan if he'd worked on it, even though the signs were all there. But we do know he designed most of the best old courses in Oregon, Washington and British Columbia, then died broke and in virtual obscurity. A lot of us think he was every bit the equal of Donald Ross, Alister Mackenzie or Stanley Thompson. It's as if you had a local architect doing the same great stuff as Corbusier and Gropius, and at the same time too, but completely under the radar. The buildings might still be there, but they've been fiddled with over the years, so no-one realizes how good they were or who designed them."

I like Sam's analogy, having myself noticed the similarities between the interwar golf course architects and the early modernist architects who were their contemporaries. After all, I was a functionary at The Largest Builder of Golf Course Communities In The West who happened to be married to an architect at The Most Conspicuously Modernist Firm In The West. If anyone could spot the parallels, that person should be me.

Both camps trace their origins to the go-go era after the First World War, when architecture's Bauhauses and Le Corbusiers started building machines for living, and golf's Rosses and

Mackenzie's began to shape courses for strategic interest and aesthetic appeal. In their parallel narratives, these Golden Ages were soon followed by Dark Ages—in the case of architecture beginning some time in the 1960s, and in golf architecture as early as the 1950s. It's a toss-up whether today's minimalist architects despise the postmodernism of the 1980s more than today's minimalist golf architects abhor the blandness of what they sometimes call the Trent Jones era. It's also difficult to judge which group is the most sanctimonious. It's one thing to be correct, it's another to be so proud of your certitude.

But if Fenwick is an example of Macan's Golden Age prowess, by the 18th green I am ready to sign on to the fan club. Sam proves to have a pretty good handle on its intricacies, fortunately, and I cruise through with a one-under 70, two or three strokes fewer than I would have shot without his help. That's low enough to get me well up the leaderboard, even though the course is only 6,600 yards long.

"The second last group tomorrow," Sam says. "Not bad for a guy with a wacko swing."

"Thanks, buddy. Know anything about either of these guys I'll be playing with?"

"I do, as it happens. Nick Myers—he's a kid going to school back east, somewhere like North Carolina. Danton Spanner: that guy is a bit of a local legend. Around your age. He was one of our juniors at Dunbar back in the '80s, a hot prospect who skipped college but stalled out on the Nationwide when it was still the Ben Hogan Tour. Spends a lot of time in Vegas now. Can't imagine what a pro golfer would do in a place like that." Sam makes it clear with his intonation that he knows exactly what a pro golfer would do in a place like that.

~ ~ ~ ~

Sam is able to fill me in a little more on Spanner today. Overnight investigation revealed that he'd been kicked out of Dunbar after he was caught stealing Rolexes and such from guys' lockers. Thus forewarned, I find it easy to pass when the pro inquires at the tee box about what kind of action we might be interested in. Myers bites, however. Just 19, and still pimply-faced, he buys Spanner's argument that as an amateur he can't accept any prize money, and so needs something to keep it interesting, right? His buddy on the bag wants in too, and between them they put up a grand. Myers is tickling the Top 200 on the Royal and Ancient's amateur ranking, and Spanner has done nothing as a touring pro, so match play with no strokes given probably looks pretty dope to the teen-agers. Spanner pulls 10 hundreds from a roll in his pinstripe pants, while bag buddy dashes off to the ATM in the clubhouse. Sam, who presents an impressive visage of incorruptible integrity, offers to hold the money. Spanner doesn't look too happy about this but has no choice except to accede.

It soon becomes apparent that I have not brought my best form to the course on this fine day. Nothing horrendous, just a failure to make really crisp shots or convert opportunities on the rare occasions when I do. On the bright side, trailing the other two by four strokes after nine, I appear to be saving myself a grand. Less brightly, I wonder if I might be playing a little better were I in on the action. Certainly the incentive seems to be working for both Myers and Spanner, who are each 2-under and tied in their match.

Soon after the turn we begin to notice Spanner ramping up his previously subtle gamesmanship. As we're standing on the short par-4 11th, he compliments Myers on his swing. "I wish I could cut my driver so reliably the way you do. It's the only way to get close on a hole like this."

Myers, who's one-up now, pulls out his driver and hits a gorgeous power fade—leaving himself a short pitch to a green that's slanted steeply away and pretty much impossible to hold, which in turn leads to an almost inevitable chip back from the other side and, ultimately, a bogey. Spanner makes a routine two-putt par after hitting a 4-iron and full wedge.

Myers bounces back with a par on 12 to the pro's bogey, but Spanner ties it up again when Myers bogeys 13 after a nervous three-putt, perhaps helped along by the pinstriper's complaints about uneven green speed. Then, on the par-3 14th, Spanner hits his ball to the front of the green, 25 feet short of the pin. I'm going third and still haven't made my club selection because of the wind, which is gusting and swirling. "Wow," Spanner says. "Didn't expect that," showing us his 7-iron. Asking for or giving advice about club selection is against the rules and would result in a two-stroke penalty in the tournament and loss of hole in the match. But advice can only be given orally, so technically Spanner is onside. Myers takes the bait, puts away his 7 and pulls out a 6. Whoops. His ball flies over the green and collects in a hollow 20 yards back. I hit my 7 and put it to five feet. "A lot of people think the advice rule is stupid," Sam says to me as we walk to the green. "But it's there to prevent players from setting each other up."

They both par 15, then Myers goes ahead with a birdie on 16. Meanwhile, we've learned that the group behind us is booting it all over the course, so suddenly the match looks to be worth quite a bit of money, for Spanner at least.

The pro has been playing more and more slowly, no doubt in an attempt to get under Myers' skin, and before the par-5 17th, tournament officials warn us that we're almost a hole behind the group in front and have been put on the clock, with penalties a possibility. But Spanner dawdles along even more deliberately, and from 60 yards out turns positively glacial, pulling out and putting back his wedges and rehearsing shots of various kinds.

Myers is in something of a panic, and after Spanner gives him a kind of wave, opts to go ahead and make his shorter pitch, leaving himself inside 10 feet.

"Hey, I'm away," yells Spanner.

"You waved me ahead."

"I don't think I made anything like a wave but if there was a gesture of some sort, it was to reassure you there's no need to worry—they never assess those penalties. Sorry about the confusion. I certainly did not wave you on. For the purposes of the match, there's no penalty, you'll just have to do it over. Just pick your ball up and deem it unplayable under penalty of stroke and distance for the tournament."

"No way."

"Or, if you want to putt out from there, feel free because there's no penalty for playing out of turn in stroke play. Of course, you'll have to concede the hole in the match."

"Come on, dude. No way."

"Here's the rule book. Let's look it up. You'll find it under 10-1c."

"You prick."

"Now, now, remember your etiquette." Sam and I look at each other. Spanner really is a prick. A prick who has the rules down cold.

After sinking his putt—an amazing feat, considering—Myers is two strokes ahead for the tournament but just even in the match. Of course, Spanner doesn't care a lot about losing the tournament to an amateur because the prize money is reserved for the pros, and winning the 18th will still get him the match even though the kid's been outplaying him.

The finishing hole at Fenwick is a mere 400-yard par-4, but it's narrow and absolutely no pushover, with a marshy hazard down the left and out of bounds to the right. Only a couple of strokes behind Spanner after running off a string of birdies, I nail one straight down the fairway while both Myers and Spanner bounce into the hazard. Myers has no choice but to take a drop, while Spanner is lucky enough to find his ball in a scruffy but playable patch of dry ground, thus disproving the concept of karma forever. Sam, who shadowed the pro closely during the search, sighs audibly when he spots the ball.

One thing Spanner can't be accused of is minimizing the slow-play issue. Not only have we caught up to the group in front, there's even a wait as they grind out what must be some pretty important putts. We are clumped closely together 130 yards out, with Spanner standing beside his ball just inside the hazard because he will be the first to hit. Sam, who has been chewing on a reedy blade of grass, passes me another one that he's fetched back from the marsh. "Hey Jeff, taste this stuff. Weird, huh, like licorice."

As I take it from him, he makes a gesture that seems closely related to Jenny's stupid look. I recognize that an appropriate response is expected, but I am still trying to decide what that might be when Sam starts talking to Spanner. "Hey Dan, am I wrong or did you just remove that blade of grass, potentially improving your area of intended swing? That's a two-stroke penalty for the tournament and loss of hole for the match. Rule 13-2, as if you didn't know."

Spanner stares at Sam with what would be described as a look of barely controlled fury, if only it were possible to pull off Blue Steel with a reed hanging from your mouth. Sam plucks the two grand out of his pocket and peels the bills to Myers, counting the sum out loud. "The guys at Dunbar send you their love," he says to Spanner. "Now spit out the grass and shoot."

~ ~ ~ ~

Jenny is in good spirits upon her return from L.A., a city that she now regards as "underrated." Her work had her spending time in Venice Beach—no, nothing to do with *Western Tractor* magazine, she assures—and the pal she stayed with lives in an apartment near the boundary of Beverly Hills and West Hollywood. She had a fine time checking out boutiques, going to galleries and eating at restaurants that regular tourists from the Pacific Northwest can't get into but her publicist buddy can. Yet this jet-setter has consented to accompany me to dinner on both Friday and Saturday, with my mom and—can I even say this?—my dad.

"You realize that with this one charitable act you have officially reimbursed me for those dozens of golf lessons billable at $125 each."

"Actually, you owe me. All those sexual services at $50 to $300 per."

"$50? What does a guy get for that?"

"Handjobs. I'm giving you the friends and family rate."

Nice to see that some of that classy L.A. attitude has rubbed off on Jenny. "Well, don't forget about the stove delivery. Halfway across town in 43 seconds."

"So that's another 74 cents."

"Which gets us to even then, I guess. Well, thank you for agreeing to accompany me on Friday and Saturday. Really appreciate it." The girl can be funny. Given my expertise on such matters, it's best to reserve judgement, but can it be that our relationship is heading, as they say, to the next level?

"But what's this I hear about a big-time golfer like you only finishing third in a piss-ant local tournament?"

"It's true. Mediocre, I know, but mediocrity of a reasonably high level."

"That's what we're all striving after, isn't it. But seriously, are you sure you don't want to be alone on the day you meet your daddy?"

"So sure that I've asked Bill along too."

"Wow. I'm flattered. So, I'm part of your posse. Cool."

"Yes, surrounding myself with all of my friends—well, both of my friends—for a family gathering. Perhaps it does indicate a certain deficiency of character—specifically, a complete lack of belief in oneself and a pitiable absence of courage. But I've always owned up to those things, haven't I? And as for sharing a place in my heart with the late-middle-aged operator of a driving range who abuses Craigslist and could stand to lose 20 pounds but also, incidentally, rescued me from the mental health slag heap, well, you should be flattered."

"And so I am. By the way, what you just said, the last bit, that's very assertive of you."

"I'm in training. For when my mom arrives."

Jenny expresses the standard view that my mother can't be so bad, as people feel they must. And seriously, what if Mom is on her best behavior, or has mellowed with time, or even—and this would be the worst—proves to be a completely pleasant and well-adjusted person who impresses everyone? Any of these, but especially the latter, would suggest it's me and not her who's the personality-disordered one.

~ ~ ~ ~

MIDORI, JULY 6

I am looking forward to this. To seeing Hiroshi and maybe also to fixing things up between us. Hector, that will be interesting too.

The genetics are much more complicated than I ever imagined. Corn we are definitely not. Even pigs are simpler to analyze, and who would sell pigs short? Is it a surprise that it would take so long for the heterosis advantage to reveal itself in Hiroshi? Maybe, maybe not. Hybrid vigor should be evident in the young. Then again, there has been no research into humans, so we can't be certain.

And yes, I must take full responsibility for the flaws in the breeding program. If I'd known then what I know now, I would have held out for the shortstop. He went on to be an executive, just like Masa's dad. A far superior match. Sure, he was a Mormon, but he was also 21. Chances are good I would have been able to convince him to help me out.

But instead I got Hector. Not the straightforward life one imagines of a baseball star, if the little I've found out is any indication. I'll spare Hiroshi the details for now, so as not to spoil the reunion.

Of course, it's possible they will bond. I hope so. There has been so much research into psychology compared to genetics. I guess that's hardly a surprise when they've had so much more money to spend. The things I could have done if we had one-tenth of that!

And what kind of science is psychology? They appear to have changed their minds on just about everything. There I was, trying to be a good mother, reading those books by Freud and Jung, and it's possible I was doing more harm than good.

That's pretty much what the psychologists are saying now. A complete about-face! At least they're acknowledging the importance of genes and biochemistry, unlike the old days. About half of the personality is nature, they admit—but the other half, the nurture half, is hardly the parents at all. Most of it comes from peers. That makes a lot of sense too. Masa spent his time with the good kids, while Hiroshi liked the goofy, lazy ones. Maybe I should have tried to do something, but I had no basis.

Anyway, the experiment is over as far as I'm concerned. Now, all that's left is for a lady to make peace with her son. Let's hope things work as I've planned.

At least I am beginning to understand him. Even when he was a baby I recognized I was at a disadvantage, knowing so little about Hector. But it turns out the father wasn't the only issuee. I should have been worrying about the peers. And yet, what could I do? It would have been hard to carry on any real research, me working those long hours at the lab, and with so little insight into the ways of this country. How could I begin to understand those kids?

But it's strange—as little as I see of Hiroshi these days, I get to observe his old friend Ian all the time. When his mother moved out my way, Ian came right along with her. And not only does he live in her basement, like he always has, but the other friend, Ben, seems to spend a lot of time visiting. Well, maybe this goes beyond science, but from observing Ian and Ben I think I've finally figured out Hiroshi. There's even a name for it. He's what's known as a slacker.

So finally, I could do some research. None of the references are very scientific, I'm afraid, but then it's psychology, right? In fact, it was the movies that were most helpful—especially the work of the directors Kevin Smith and Judd Apatow. What a revelation! I feel like I know my own son for the first time. I can even speak his language.

"Hiroshi! Give your mom a hug."

"How was your trip?"

"The trip was cool. It's so great that we get to hang out together."

"Right."

"But, Jeffrey—is that what they call you, or Jeff?"

"Jeff is fine."

"Cool. I just want this weekend to be about you and your dad."

"Well, you too."

"No, it's not about me. For me Hector was just a one-night stand. Not even that. A quick hook up!"

"Mom?"

"Actually, not so quick. He couldn't get it up. Friends without benefits!"

"Mom?"

"It's true. But this is your chance to have a father."

"OK…"

"So I think the itinerary is starting to make some sense. You meet him in an hour at the bar at the restaurant. It's a cool place. I checked it out online. Now, look, it's just going to be the two of you until dinner. I know I said I'd be there, but it's best if you get to know each other first. He said he'd wear a blue golf shirt and a hat."

"I know what Hector looks like."

"Cool—the baseball pictures. But he was younger then. I'm not even sure I'll recognize him, and I …"

"No, I've seen him in person."

What do you mean? When could you have seen him?

"When I was in Nicaragua in 1990. He was speaking at a rally and I went and saw him."

"Your dad? Why didn't you introduce yourself?"

"I don't know. Shyness. Cowardice."

"You know what, dude? It's time you got over that."

~ ~ ~ ~

JEFF

Ah, the best-laid plans. Am I here to meet someone named Hector? Well, he just called the restaurant to say he has been unavoidably delayed. He'll be arriving at 6, which will be right when the rest of the circus troops in. I have to give mom some credit for recognizing that he and I should have a few minutes together first. Too bad it isn't going to work out.

But I wonder what she's been smoking at the active adult community. Clearly being there has affected her in some mind-boggling way. When we designed those things, at least some of us tried to think about how people might actually live in them. True, even for us idealists, it was more about pushing the buttons that would have potential buyers salivating over the lifestyle, if I may be forgiven that Panglossian term. But the weird thing is, surveys and even academic research consistently turn up a high satisfaction level among residents. People reported that they were indeed more active and spent more time with others, and that these others proved to be generally agreeable and like-minded. Not quite the Utopia I planned to someday design back in grad school, but hey.

And it's funny, I have a spy there. Ian moved right along with his mom when she decamped to Shangri-latte, as he calls it. And he doesn't even seem to hate the place. Even though there's only one other person under the age of 40, and she's an overly manicured trophy wife who he says has been hinting to him about her availability for clandestine get-togethers.

Ian's a different kind of guy—one of the two or three humans who made a point of keeping in touch with me during my troubles. He reads as the classic slacker, but he says the app that he and Ben have been toiling over all these years will finally hit the market in a matter of days. It was originally going to be strictly for Crackberries, but Ben has Apple connections, and a few months ago they developed a version for the iPhone thing that was released last week. Probably a smart move, if all that commotion wasn't just hype. Judging from his Facebook posts, Ian's about as stoked as a Jack Johnson fan can get. They've been demoing it around, and have already turned down an $8 million investment from a venture capital firm that wanted too big a stake. I hope he can last one more week before caving in to the trophy wife, because it looks like his vistas will soon extend beyond his ground-level view of a graveled-over back yard.

And what of my vistas? Ian may have been slow to launch, but his trajectory figures to be impressive. Meanwhile, I was carefully designed for maximum performance and have completely failed to attain it. At best I'd call myself a misunderstood Zeppelin, stalwart and useful, but prone to explosion. Others no doubt think more along the lines of the VZ-9 Avrocar, a flying saucer thing designed in the 1950s to travel through the skies at 300 mph but sadly capable of making it only three feet off the ground. If every hybrid were like me, the world would be starving. Then again, as my suddenly surprising mom says, maybe it's time to get over that, dude.

And now, suddenly, there's a 60-year-old black guy in a blue golf shirt walking toward me as if he knows who I am. It must be my father because he is as socially awkward as I am. Yes, he looks pretty much as he did 16 years ago, and yes too, he is trying to decide whether to shake my hand or attempt a familial hug, just as I am. Ultimately we both decide to go for the hybrid version, no irony intended—the classic handshake-leading-into-a-shoulder-clasp-and-then-a-brief-interlude-of-hand-on-the-back.

"It is Hiroshi, correct?"

"Call me Jeff, Hector, and what a pleasure."

And thus ends the touching encounter of lost father and son, because into the restaurant parades the entire retinue, on time to a person: Bill and Jenny together, then Mom six seconds behind. There is a moment of clumsy shuffling as introductions are made, but both Jenny and Bill are socially accomplished and quickly sort us out while pointing the conversation in an appropriate direction. Mom wondered why I was so insistent on dragging Bill along, but his value quickly becomes apparent, as he smoothly arranges us around the table, with Hector in the position of honor, flanked by Mom and me.

Hector will have only one drink, he says, and Bill takes matters in hand to make it Champagne, the real stuff. Then, after toasts are made and meals ordered, the table miraculously quiets, leaving Hector and me to converse.

"Can I ask a question about your baseball career?" Perhaps Hector and I will become more intimate at some future date. But here, talking to a quasi-celebrity I have never met and with others listening in, I am behaving more in the manner of someone hosting a program on NPR.

"Of course."

"Well, I know how good you were. I checked your stats. But how come you changed teams so often? Even leagues and countries."

"For me this is an awkward question, but I will answer. I have, I guess you would say, a temper. I was never a helmet thrower. On the ball field things are not so important, but sometimes in my personal life, well, I react."

"Sure, we all do."

"Yes, but I react more strongly. I have been told that my flight or fight response is very highly attuned. My father was like that as well. Perhaps it is in the genes." Jenny and mom both fail in their attempt to avoid glancing at me. Bill, to his credit, succeeds.

"So, you say you have a temper."

"Yes, and sometimes I could not control it. Sometimes I even hurt people. It was not something that filled me with pride."

"You hurt people?"

"Yes, perhaps I hit them, or there was a baseball bat." For all his reserve and formality, Hector is not doing a good job of hiding behind them. "Sometimes they would try to run away, but that just made me angrier. Maybe you will believe me when I tell you that no-one has ever outrun Hector Ramon. No-one."

"Oh, I believe you. But that wasn't why you left here, was it?"

"No, but it is true that sometimes I had to move to another city. Or, as you say, to another country. However, all that was many years ago. I have learned to control my temper, and of course in Miami my life is very different."

"You live in Miami?"

"Oh, you did not know that? I moved many years ago. 1995. I have dual citizenship now. Nicaragua and America."

"What do you do in Miami?"

"I have dedicated myself to fitness and health. I am a partner in a gym, and my duties include reaching out to the community. Perhaps you have been there and have seen for yourself how people take care of themselves, how heavy they are. I am not too modest to state that I have established myself as a role model."

A role model—is this the moment to bring up Hector's less than savory side, his time as a cocaine-peddling, peasant-killing Contra? Is there a way to do this with some sensitivity? The brain is still considering the question when the lips begin to move. "I seem to recall that you were a Contra working with Oliver North. That must have been exciting."

"A Contra? Oliver North? No, that is a mistake."

How strange that my own father would fail to take responsibility for his actions. "You weren't involved in the elections in 1990?"

"Oh, the elections, certainly. Violeta is a friend of mine. A wonderful woman who brought peace to the country."

"She wasn't with the Contras?"

"She was with the Sandinistas until their intentions became clear. She was an important part of their government. Then she joined the coalition that defeated them in the elections. The first woman to defeat a sitting male president anywhere in the world. A hero that I am proud to have served!"

Hector's interpretation of central American politics would have to be given at least as much credence as a barroom full of First World 20-somethings exceptionally well-versed in the alternative music scene. And it is my recollection from following Nicaragua's progress upon returning to my studies that Chamorra turned out to be a strong and reasonable president. So now, let's see how deftly Jeff, the budding broadcaster, can shift this conversation back on track.

"A role model. Yes, I don't think I've ever seen a man of 60 look so fit." Hector and I are both careful not to look over at the other 60-year-old man at our table, but then I begin to worry that our circumspection is in fact a form of rebuke, so I attempt to lighten the mood. "Maybe you should be reaching out to the community here as well. Some of us could use a role model."

Hector accepts this as a simple statement. "Well, I am. On Sunday I will be racing here. I will be attempting to set a new world record in the 200 meters for my over-60 age class. The record has stood since 1994. Twenty-four seconds even. But I think I can run it in 23:90, maybe even 23:80. I believe it will be the first world record ever held by a Nicaraguan."

"Wow. A world record. I didn't know there were Masters games here this weekend."

"Not the Masters Games," my mother interrupts. "The *Gay* Games, right?"

"Yes, that is correct. It would also be the first world record ever set by an out homosexual. I cannot guarantee that I will break the record, of course, but I have been working toward this moment for two years. And if I am successful, it will be an important statement. Media around the world have been alerted, and many will be in attendance."

I am momentarily nonplussed. Hector is gay? I suppose I should be grateful that I have been spared the awkward, "There's something I have to tell you," coming out speech. "So, right. I guess I didn't realize that you are gay."

"Yes, I'm gay. I have known since I was 11. In fact, I have always believed it to be a miracle that I was able to conceive a son." Mom's on her best behavior but she permits herself a grin that can only be described as smug.

"That must have been another thing that interfered with your baseball career." Now I have decided to be the dull-witted sportscaster, resolutely determined to keep the conversation focused on sporting matters when the interviewee wants to talk about something important.

"It was not so bad. Ball players were no less prejudiced than anyone else in those days, but they wanted to win, and fortunately, I could help them do that. I tried to make my own life, and I stayed away from other players except at the ballpark. I learned that lesson here."

"How do you mean?"

"Despite what some gay people think, there are not many of us in professional sports, but here there was one, and I could see that. We had a relationship, but he was conflicted—he believed that homosexuality was wrong and that he could change. He told the manager that I had assaulted him, and I was advised to never show my face in America again."

"So that's why you left town so quickly."

"Yes, I wanted to stay here because I had a son."

"That's tragic, for me as well as you." I doff my yellow blazer for a few seconds before putting it back on again. "And what became of the other guy?"

"He got married soon after and had a good career. Now he's vice-president of a major corporation."

"The shortstop," Mom says.

"Yes, the shortstop." Hector glances toward Mom, who seems to have done some research. "The year after he retired he left his wife, and now he lives as a homosexual. I have helped him with advice and support."

"That must hurt."

"Not really. I understand why he did it. My life has been good. It might have been different, but it has been good nonetheless."

The table is silent as everyone digests the implications of Hector's courage and sacrifice. The silence lasts for nanoseconds,

seconds even. Then someone says something unimportant, and we begin to babble in a manner more typical of our species. It is 9 o'clock before we leave, and then only because of the curfew set by Hector's trainer.

~ ~ ~ ~

"What's that song?

"What do you mean, song?"

"The one you're whistling."

"Oh, I'm whistling. Just something I must have heard on the radio. Guess it's that Feist tune."

"Great night for a whistle. You must be thrilled."

"It is pretty cool. I have a daddy."

"And you know what? Hector may be a bit of a project, but the apple didn't fall far from the tree. Hey, I have some news, too. Remember the phone call I had to take?"

"Oh, yeah. What was that about?"

"Well, hang onto your hat—I'm moving to L.A. I have a new job!"

"So you weren't researching an article."

"I guess I wasn't."

"But that's great, right? I'm happy for you." I think I am succeeding in my attempt not to look like a sad puppy dog.

"I knew you would be. You're not going to believe this, but it's a golf magazine. A new one. Golf, wine, real estate, a bit of fashion—very 21st century. It's going to be way upscale, for all those people who are living the life in a house on the golf course, but without being too, too Republican." My eyebrows involuntarily rise when I hear a political reference from Jenny, even one that can only be described as neutral and allusional. I think she's a little too paranoid about this kind of stuff, but she swears that as a supposedly objective magazine journalist it would be career suicide to reveal that she has ever thought about choosing one side over the other, or indeed has ever thought very deeply about anything.

"That is great."

"I couldn't have done it without you. I wouldn't have known anything about golf, obviously. I knew I had them when I started explaining minimalist design. Can you believe they didn't know about the Golden Age? Or even Stack & Tilt!"

"How long have you known about this *opportunity?*"

"A couple of months, I guess. An old friend from J-school works at one of their other magazines and she mentioned there might be something in the pipe."

"So early May. Just before we met."

"I guess that's right."

"Just before you answered my ad offering free golf instruction."

"Yeah—but hey! I didn't place that ad. I wasn't the one out trawling."

"But you put two and two together."

"Look, I knew I had to learn something about golf. But you were the one employing the Bill gambit—impress the chick as the precise opposite of a skirt chaser, with the explicit intention of getting into her pants. Which you pulled off to perfection!"

"I couldn't pull off anything, you know that."

"And yet you did. My pants, followed seconds later by my underwear, if you'll recall. Because that's what successful people who don't want to spend the rest of their lives hitting bucket after bucket on someone's driving range do. They figure out a way for their self-interest to sync up with the self-interest of other people."

Perhaps not an insight of Newtonian proportions, but one that would have to be given some consideration. Maybe Hector isn't the only one in the family who can rise to an occasion. "I know it isn't like me, but I'm going to be big here and buy at least part of that," I say. "Hey, here's a thought. Couldn't do it right away, or even really soon, but maybe I could follow you down there."

"Oh, Jeff, that's so sweet. Sure, who knows, but let's just take things as they come."

"As in, let's keep our options open."

"Yes, you have my permission to pollute the public good that is Craigslist with your unconscionable strategies."

"But that's not what I want to do. I want to be with you. Except that you're dumping me."

"Sweetie, I'm not dumping you. We've been great together, and you're a treat, but we have to be practical."

"I am being practical. I'm really starting to get attached to you."

"And me to you, but there's so much to think about. I'm only 32, remember?"

"Yeah, so six years between us. No big deal."

"Well, I haven't given up on having kids."

"Just because we haven't talked about kids doesn't mean I don't want them. I do want kids. Especially after this evening."

"But that's not us."

"What do you mean?"

"Well, when I have kids I have an idea of what they'll, you know, look like."

"Are you saying what I think you're saying? That you're OK to sleep with Mandingosan, but not to breed with him?"

"Nothing to do with race. Everyone has an idea of what they're looking for in a mate. Tall, not too heavy, whatever. Genes—as if I need to tell you, of all people. For example, almost everyone is wary of a history of ridiculously stupid and insane behavior, but I'm letting you off the hook on that one. I just want kids who look like me, that's all."

Suddenly I feel like The Hulk. Why is it so hard for Hulk to think? "I'm going home," I say. "We can talk tomorrow."

~ ~ ~ ~

But we're not going to talk today. Or maybe ever again. Upon waking from a less than fitful sleep, I email her: "You're off the hook for tonight." She responds, "When can we talk?" I turn off my cell phone and neglect to answer the email.

Bill is in his office when I finish with my 9 o'clock group. "In for a few minutes?" he asks.

"Half an hour till the next group."

"Sit down then. There's something I have to tell you. A couple of things to talk about, actually."

"Yeah?"

"You know I've been worried about the business this year."

"Yeah."

"I'm not worried any more."

"That's good."

"Maybe not so good. I just sold it."

"Our business?"

"No, we'll get to that. The range."

"Really?"

"Yeah, the offer came out of nowhere, and you won't believe who. Fitzpatrick, the Pontiac-Buick dealer, is looking to expand. The past few years have been lights out for the car business, as you probably know. Not so much for GM, it's true, but he thinks Pontiac has turned it around, and is headed for the stars. Between you and me, I'm not really buying that. But you're not going to believe which GM marque really is doing pretty well."

"Maybe La Salle?" Somehow, the notoriously slow-thinking Jeff Jones has remembered the name of the last GM marque before Oldsmobile to face corporate execution, a Cadillac near clone that was done in just before the Second World War when it became clear GM would be better off making military vehicles than overstyled luxury cars.

"That's probably more the case than they'd like to admit. But I kid you not, Saab-Saturn. At least around here. Well enough that the city's getting another franchise, and he's been given it. So he decided to pick up my land and move both dealerships here."

"So, no more driving range. Away go the Oldsmobiles and in come the Saabs. Cute. And worth some pretty good money, if I may be so bold."

"Quite a bit. Just over three million. Three times what I paid. Caught this real estate bubble pretty close to the top, I think. I still have some old debts to make good on, but I'll do OK."

"You said we would talk about our business?"

"Yeah, well, it looks like I'm going to head off to Denmark for a few months."

"That's such a great thing for you to do. What a smart choice. You so deserve it."

"Anyway, it means I won't be around to run the Stack & Tilt business."

"So, who will?"

"You can always find someone else, but realistically there's no reason why it couldn't be a one-man show."

"Run everything myself?"

"Yeah, just buy me out, and away you go."

"How do you mean?"

"How do I mean, what?"

"Buy me out?"

"It's a partnership. We each own half the business, and we each have to be able to sell our shares. There's a procedure. It's all laid out in the partnership agreement that you signed. You read that, right?"

"Of course. Maybe not so carefully. Well, maybe not all of it. OK, a lot of it was just boilerplate, wasn't it?"

"If by boilerplate you mean carefully spelled out in a thoroughly considered and legally binding form, yes."

This is getting a little frightening.

"Don't worry. The value of our shares is dependent on metrics that can't be calculated yet—revenues and profitability, mostly. Right now we're on target for $180,000 in revenues on an annualized basis, but that will only happen if the marketing effort continues to be aggressive. Plus, right now our labor is the primary expense, but you'll probably have to spend more on overhead and hire some help without me here. So you won't owe me a lot—maybe 30 grand."

"Uh, OK."

"And I'm not looking to sell just yet. Who knows, I may want to jump back in. So if you want to keep me in and pay me a dividend and maybe a consulting fee, that's fine. Or if you want to buy me out, I'll listen to offers."

"I'll take the former, thanks."

"Good. Something else you need to hear about."

"Fire away."

"Well, you know what you said your mom loving Denmark?"

"Yes, I guess I did say that." Something is very wrong with the direction this conversation seems to be headed, and I fear that I will soon learn the extent of its excruciating wrongness.

"Anyway, we're going there together."

"You're going to Denmark with…"

"Your mom. She knows the country and wants to go back."

"And this all happened last night."

"Yeah, great lady. Very open to experiences…"

Bill has generously shared many of his late night experiences with me, often employing vivid details that betray his status as a charter subscriber to *Penthouse Forum*. "I'm sure Denmark has changed a lot," I interrupt.

"I wouldn't know. Never been there."

"What do you mean? That's where you're from."

"My parents are from there. They got out during the war."

"But all your connections…"

"There wasn't money for travel when I was a kid, and then I was always working. Most of the family left, so there weren't a lot of cousins or anything like that. Saab was going to send me to Sweden once, but something came up. So I've never been to Europe."

"But all the art, and furniture. All those details…"

"Everyone knows about Danish furniture. It's the world's best, available anywhere. The paintings, I just used an agent. General knowledge—you ever hear of books? The internet?"

"I guess. But I am surprised. And my mom—you like her apparently?"

"I do. Maybe because she's so much like you."

"What's that, your impression of the form Danish humor might hypothetically take?"

"No, she's like you. Intelligent and creative. Maybe not so good with people."

"Keep going. You've only narrowed it down to maybe 10 percent of the population, and it's hard to see either of us being that normal." I am definitely being a little sharp with Bill. Am I annoyed that he seems to see something in my mom that I have missed? Am I hurt that he appears to have chosen her over me? Or am I merely pressing my advantage, now that he has revealed himself to suffer, not from mere nostalgia, but from that rarest of perversions, entirely irrational Scandiphilia?

"Well, all that focus. You've told me your mom is prone to enthusiasms, but isn't it better to care too much rather than too little? To pursue something too far instead of not far enough? Could you have developed your swing if you weren't a little obsessive? And both of you are so emotional. You try to suppress it but you can't—you're the definition of sensitive. Your mom, she had to learn to hide her emotions. A scientist with radical ideas and a woman in a man's world to boot—she had to act tough even though she isn't. And when people try to be something they're not, the real stuff always leaks out. That's one of the reasons she seemed like such a weird mom.

Weird mom—can't argue with that analysis. My annoyance with Bill has receded sufficiently that I am giving serious consideration to buying the new 9.5 that he is figuratively trying to sell me, the SportWagon version.

"And the intensity. You were born on the west coast and absorbed enough of the laid back thing from your peers that you can pass for normal most of the time. Your mom grew up in Japan—only now is she starting to realize that we're suspicious here of people who are too intense."

A sunroof for only $29.99 more a month? Of course I'd take that.

"Look at yourself. You need a manager, right? You suffered from a classic case of failure to launch until Syd came along and everything started to head in the right direction. Things didn't go so well without her there, then look at what happened when you hooked up with me."

Thank you, Bill, for not going into intricate detail about what I get up to when not being expertly administered, and yes, I will spring for the audio upgrade.

"Well, your mom never found her manager. She was a single mom with two young boys, and one of those boys was always a little lost. She loved her work and wanted to put in the same long hours as everyone else, but she was torn because she was needed at home. Except, she wasn't very good at home and didn't know how to get better. And that caused stress, and she's not good with stress."

If Bill is attempting to not only impart understanding but help me get to a place where I feel for my mom, well, it's working—and absolutely I'll take the extended warranty.

"Well, now she's going to have a manager, for at least a few months. And yes, I really do like your mom. You've always assumed that I'm perfectly content as the, you know, playboy. But you're not someone who really thinks about what makes other people tick. Sorry, but it's true. If you did think about it, you'd probably get it wrong anyway. So would your mom—that's the way you are.

"I play the crowd because I've never found someone who made we want to do otherwise. With your mom, something happened, some sort of instant recognition. I've just turned 60 and for the first time in my life I feel like I've met someone that I really know. Maybe, like I said, because I know you."

What I'll do with two 9.5s is beyond me, but Bill has made the sale. Do I believe that he is done with the swordsman's life? Not really. But is it concerning that a man with a wandering eye and the guile of a gypsy (and I don't mean to offend any gypsies) will be accompanying my mother on a European vacation? Not at all. Regardless of what he says, I happen to know that my mom can take care of herself. Indeed, at some point Bill is probably going to discover the limits of his ability to read a person like a book. That said, Mom deserves whatever happiness she gets from him, for as long as it lasts. "I'm happy for you, then. And for my mom, too. Especially my mom."

"Good. I wouldn't want it otherwise, you know that. You have to head out to the range now, but let's find some time to talk again soon. The sale closes in 10 days and we're leaving right after that. We need to get you set up at another facility."

"Indeed we do. Are you around this afternoon? My dad's coming in at 3 to learn all about Stack & Tilt."

"Sorry, I'm spending some time with this hot chick I just met. But I know you'll have fun and so will I."

"OK, Bill. Be absolutely certain to spare me the juicy details."

~ ~ ~ ~

In the past 18 hours I have been dumped by my girlfriend and my business partner. The former proved to be a closet racist;

the latter turns out to own half of my teaching career and will shortly be splitting for Denmark, along with both my livelihood and my mom—who is apparently a wonderful woman that I completely misunderstood and have been selling tragically short for the past 38 years.

And yet I am whistling. No doubt this is because in a few minutes I will greet my long lost father, who will be dropping by to sample the fine art of Stack & Tilt. Oh, he's not perfect. That became abundantly clear last night. But he's mine, all mine, and those imperfections of his go a long way to clearing up the reasons behind some of my own.

I have never tidied a driving range stall before, but here I am wondering if there is a correct way to place a chair. Dad's gay, after all, so he'll have an overly developed sense of how such things should be turned out.

"Hey, Jeff. Sure you got that right?"

Steve Milbrandt, one of my students, is hitting balls a few stalls down, and he's making an effort to be friendly. "A VIP coming in. Have to make sure everything's just so."

"I hear you. I always like to center my mat in the stall. Feng shui, right?"

"Right," I say, taking care to show appreciation for what I believe Steve feels is a clever little joke. And thanks, Steve, for the suggestion. An excess of symmetry isn't in keeping with modernist ideals, but what can a modernist do with a square mat, in any case? Shouldn't there be rectangular mats for us? Are the golf supply companies not aware of the Golden Mean? And is Hector even a modernist? Latin America didn't suffer the anti-modern backlash in the same way. Plus he is gay, so yes, probably. Still, let's center the mat and see how it looks. Actually, kind of good. There.

"Dad!"

"I am pleased to see you, Jeff."

"You slept well, I hope."

"I certainly did. Subsequently I engaged in a light workout as prescribed by my trainer, and ate a lunch in keeping with the schedule laid out my nutritionist. Now I am ready to have my golf swing diagnosed and corrected by the renowned golf coach, Jeff Jones. I am lucky to be in such good hands."

"Indeed you are. That was fun last night. A very good time."

"The memories will be preserved forever."

"So I've set you up here with some clubs. Warm up as you like, and then let's watch you take a few swings."

Watching Hector warm up with a 9-iron, I can't help but be struck by his athleticism and fitness level. Wow. For someone who golfs only a few times a year, that is a powerful looking swing. A little outside, perhaps, and the tempo could be better, but it's easy enough to see why he can just pick up the clubs and shoot in the low 80s. We begin with some minor adjustments to grip, stance and alignment, then I have Hector put away his iron and pull out the driver, in keeping with my now thoroughly proven approach.

"If you've taken lessons before, this might seem odd, but I believe that students can get a better feel for this swing with their drivers."

"I place my trust in you with full conviction."

"Now I want you to feel loose, and I'm looking for a big swing. Not fast but wide. The difference from your regular swing is, I want you to keep your back leg straight and to feel like almost all your weight is on the front. You're going to rotate around that leg. You're going to feel like you're grinding that leg into the ground, and you're going to let your momentum carry you through into a very full follow-through." I demonstrate with a slightly exaggerated rotation and follow-through.

Hector tries some abbreviated half-speed versions of what I'm asking for, much as if he were swinging in the on-deck circle. I can see him testing the new sensation of winding around the leg instead of shifting his weight from leg to leg. It's such a treat to watch a natural athlete in action.

Now he is ready to step up and take a real swing at the ball teed up on the mat. I'd asked for a big swing, and wow, does he deliver. Huge extension and a really big turn for a guy who's in his 60s. Back goes the clubhead, stopping just above the horizon, then looping slightly farther behind him for the return trip. This is shaping up to be a very nice swing except—*clang*!

I am briefly confused as to what might have happened, then it all becomes clear. Hector's swing was so wide, and the mat so centered, that the clubhead snagged the stall divider behind him as he was bringing it back around. Somehow, Hector lost his balance as a result and is now prone on the mat.

"Oh!" he says. "*Joder! Joder! Puta madre!*" After all these years my Spanish is vestigial at best, but it's good enough to recognize that Hector can be a lot more colloquial in his first language than his second.

Steve, who's a physiotherapist, has rushed over to see if he can be of any help. Hector is now on one knee, but he is holding his right shoulder, and Steve quickly determines that it has been injured.

"I've got some bad news," he says. "That shoulder is…"

"I know," I interrupt. "Save your breath. It's fucking separated."

CHAPTER 7
DRIVER OFF THE DECK

JULY 27, 2007

There will be no Oldsmobiles at Dunbar Gates today; probably not in the parking lot, and certainly not on the golf course. Those old land barges served a purpose—two-ton anchors that helped secure a guy at constant risk of drifting away and maybe even under. But on the morning that Bill and I stood and watched Cutlass after Cutlass being towed to the wrecker, I came to the realization that I no longer needed that kind of help. Playing in the club championship this weekend I won't need to concentrate on a course that I know every inch of, or on a game that I know is rock solid. So, hell (note to self: use this retro-cool word more often), might as well let the mind wander.

I can begin by contemplating the situation with the women in my life, not to mention my dad. It can fairly be said that circumstances at the driving range took on a slapstick quality during the seconds after Hector's accident and Steve's diagnosis of a separated shoulder. First there was the explosion of Spanish curse words, impressive to say the least, and yet not a sufficient venting mechanism, to judge from what came next. It's no wonder Hector led league after league in doubles, considering the way he bent those clubs into raw material for an Alexander Calder mobile, and with only one good arm, too.

But after destroying almost the entire set of Bill's best rentals, he seemed to undergo a change of expression. Jenny said it struck her as a Homeric moment, and she wasn't talking about *The Odyssey* but rather *The Simpsons*, specifically the family breadwinner's propensity in early episodes to regularly fly into a Bart-beating rage. It was the 20th century, after all, and one's juvenile offspring were viewed as mere proto-humans entirely beholden to their parents' emotions and whims.

"You cocksucker," Hector enunciated, an epithet that had perhaps been directed his way once or twice. "How can I race now?" The bag beside him was all but empty, so at least he was spared the ordeal of club selection.

As a high-school hurdler who made it to State a couple of times, I liked my chances against every other 60-year-old alive, but even with his shoulder hanging, Hector figured to be a formidable pursuer. That didn't stop me from sprinting out onto the range, stepping as dexterously as a blinding flash of light can in an attempt to avoid the carpet of balls accumulating due to Bill's ball-picker having called in sick. Dozens of people were standing in their stalls, no doubt marveling at my athleticism as I leapt onto and over the Cutlass Calais Supreme—blue, of course—parked at 200 yards. Or perhaps they were gawking at the grey-haired Hector, who was mere steps behind, seven-iron in hand (the ultimate multi-purpose club after all), until 160 yards out, when his foot found a ball, turning his ankle and landing him in another heap. I stood behind the Olds as first Jenny and then my mom ran out toward him. Jenny was clearly trying to calm my father, who now had a sprained ankle to go with his separated shoulder, but my mom appeared to have a different intent. Swinging her handbag like a coked-up street hooker, she bashed him on the head once, then again, then yet again, before Bill himself could get out there and restrain her. I hadn't previously been aware of any athletic inclinations on my mom's part, but at 62 she still looked as if she could have played any sport she wanted. It's sad that so many women are deprived of athletic pursuits due to social pressures.

Finally, with Steve administering medical attention, the group convinced Hector to stop his whimpering and got him onto his feet, or, realistically, foot. Then together they limped him out of the range and into Steve's car. A couple of teenaged miscreants were already starting to fire their range balls at me, but only when Hector was out of sight did I leave the Cutlass, which I believed I'd be able to duck around and over in the event he resumed the chase and proved able to outrun me in a straight line.

Yet, was I contrite? Apparently not, as my first question to Jenny upon her return wasn't "How's Hector?" but "What are you doing here?" After all, I'd vowed never to talk to her again, even though I'd yet to pass the message along.

"I knew you'd be here from last night, and I wanted to talk, but I'm not sure this is the best time."

Then my mom came running over—*running*—and began fussing over me, checking that everyone was OK. "That prick," she said. "Bill said there was something wrong with him. I thought maybe it was just the gay thing, and Bill being such a straight guy, but what a fuckwit."

"Mom?" I asked, no longer able to keep my counsel about her strange new identity. "First, who are you, and second, what are you doing here?"

"First," Jenny said, "she's a wonderful woman who took her responsibilities as a parent a little too seriously. And second, I called Bill the moment the accident happened. I guess they were close by."

"In his office," said my mom, who looked happy and surprised to have someone younger take her side for perhaps the first time in her life.

So then I had both of them doing the mothering thing. I suppose in some ways I hadn't comported myself very well, running away from Hector like that. Then again, he had talked at some length about his inability to stay in one town for very long, owing to anger management issues typically manifested in a tendency to try to kill people that he believed had done him wrong.

Jenny seemed to read my mind. "You did exactly the right thing. But I had no idea you were that fast. Wow." She looked at me in a way I had never seen before. I completely knew why too. If the adrenaline had been running like that back in highschool, I would have won the state final easily.

Mom piped in. "Why wouldn't he be? His dad was going to race for a world record, and I used to run as a girl, too. Plus," she said, "there's the hybrid vigor." Mom looked over, waiting for my face to cloud over, and started to laugh, leaving me no choice but to do likewise. Jenny joined in, and suddenly it seemed very difficult to maintain a grudge against either of them.

So Mom and I turned into a standard-issue happy family for the couple of days that she hung around before heading home to pack for Denmark. And Jenny and I became friends and, yes, lovers again. I absolved her of racism, and she absolved me of being an immature passive-aggressive, while pressing upon me the conviction that, although I might have had a weird upbringing on top of being saddled with some of the wonkiest genes ever stirred together, I wasn't a helpless captive to any of it. When the time came to catch the plane to L.A., it was me who saw her off. We would correspond and maybe even pine a little, we agreed, but we wouldn't let any of that hold us back from whatever came next.

And what in fact came next was my encounter with a representative of the fifth estate. Jenny knew that I'd already had two bad media experiences, enduring first the ineptitude of Dan Kessler, then the bile and bias of Angie Dolan. This time her cherished profession would come through for me, she promised before she left, and I can't say she was wrong. Bill had already told me to expect to hear from a reporter; our lawyer's letter and subsequent negotiations had been fruitful, and the paper was eager to publish a feature on the exciting new Stack & Tilt swing and instructor Jeff Jones, who had become a rookie sensation on the local tournament circuit since switching over. (I omit the numerous exclamation marks implied by Bill's original description.) Still, I was surprised when the reporter turned out to be Angie Dolan.

"I know you're probably suspicious of me," she said when she called. "But there's no need. The paper and I are convinced that what you're doing is real and impressive. I'll explain what happened last time when we connect in person."

She was as happy to meet at the club as at the range, which suited me, given that the Tivoli Golf and Learning Center had less than a week to live, and my new range-to-be did not yet seem like home ground. "You're a golfer?" I said. "Well, bring along your clubs."

After the ritual handshake the reporter apologized for her original article. "I realized right away that I'd been given some misleading information, and that the piece wasn't an accurate depiction," she said. "I had some pressure on the home front, if you know what I mean."

"He is your husband, then. How's the wrist?"

"Better, but he still can't swing a club."

"That's too bad." I said this in a voice intended to conceal my gleeful satisfaction.

"So," she said, after we'd teed off. "Tell me about Stack & Tilt"

Angie had done her homework: she'd asked around and read the original *Golf Digest* article and all the blogs and follow-ups in its wake. And she was smart, so this wasn't like dealing with the idiot Kessler. She took notes as I drove the cart down Dunbar's fairways for perhaps the second time in my life. The course is named after a primitive links east of Edinburgh, and we attempt to channel the Scots as much as possible, so it's almost a condition of membership that buggies will be used only under extraordinary circumstances. The things are typically seen only on the dozen or so days a year when the place is rented out for corporate tournaments.

A half-inch taller than me, and swinging men's clubs, Angie turned out to be not just an eight handicap and appealing golf companion but a limber, all-around athlete who got into sports writing after playing on both the soccer and volleyball teams at college. We were at the far corner of the darkening and deserted course when she began to talk about the story she would have to write. "In the business we call an article like this a blow-job," she said. "But I think I can go one better. You're divorced, right?"

"Right."

"Girlfriend?"

"There was someone, but she just moved away."

"Well, it turns out my asshole husband has had a girlfriend all these years," she said. "Almost got me fired, and then when I need him most he's over at her place. Well, fuck him."

But that's not who she fucked, at least not literally. "You don't mind, do you?" she asked, putting her hand on my lap. I didn't need to say anything. Women don't ask for sex very often, and it's a man's role to accommodate if he can. Everyone understands that, even my father, who fulfilled what was requested of him even though it didn't come naturally.

With the grace of an athlete, she was climbing onto me even as I slid over on the seat to avoid the wheel. The position was surprisingly comfortable, and effective too, for Angie as well as me. Especially for her. So this is what golf carts are good for, I found myself thinking.

In this inspired way one legal entanglement disappeared, officially resolved two days later when the glowing article was published, turning Bill's last day of work into a marathon of phone answering and rustproof-undercoat selling. He was surprised at the high proportion of callers who were female, which had me doubting that such a perceptive guy had even read the story, which seemed to be full of subliminal messages. Well, somewhat subliminal. One person at least was meant to understand the references to my "erect stance," "smooth stroke" and "penetrating ball-flight," and no doubt his wrist was throbbing as a result.

Regrettably, though, the newspaper's place on our legal docket had already been superseded. On the day after Hector's unfortunate accident and subsequent meltdown, a courier had arrived with a letter. "I was expecting this," said Bill, before even opening it. "But not so soon."

Sure enough, Hector was suing us. "He's quick on his feet, I'll give him that," said Bill, who explained that in less than 24 hours Hector had somehow found the very firm he himself would retain if he were pursuing someone for $7.2 million in damages over such minor injuries, all self-inflicted and with no evidence of negligence. Bill raised an eyebrow when he said this. How it happened I can't explain, but a moment after he and mom arrived on the scene, the mat Hector had been using seemed to have shifted back to its normal place, and Bill had his brand new iPhone out, taking pictures.

It was nothing to fret about, he assured me. "This is why I've been pissing away thousands of dollars a year on liability insurance. Leave the worrying to the insurance company. It's their problem now. You were just doing your job in a completely professional manner. How he could have hit that partition is a mystery that may never be solved."

Yes, Bill, let's hope. Fortunately, nothing bothers me unduly these days, so strong is my mental state. How else to explain being four under through the first 36 holes while screening a movie like this in my head? But there is more golf to be played. Among the many elegant features at Dunbar Gates is the format of the club championship, which extends to 54 holes in just two days, with the proviso that only those within five strokes of the lead make the final cut for Sunday afternoon play. There are about 80 of us gathered in the shade in front of the big scoreboard by the clubhouse, munching on sandwiches and watching as the results of the morning round are posted. Three guys at 145 are holding their breaths, hoping that my 140 stands up for the lead as the last two groups come in, but it appears that they will be disappointed. A murmur goes through the crowd that someone has just shot a 68 for a 139 total, so the cut will move to 144. A minute or two later, more numbers go up on the board and the rumor is confirmed. The new score has been posted by—yes, that's his name—by Kevin Howell.

So there will be six of us. The threesome of Dave Smart, Hugh Collingwood and Stanley Brunst will head out first, followed by the three leaders: Kevin, me and—could it be?—none other than the geriatric Stack & Tilter, Sam London.

We see the first group out, shaking their hands as they gather on the tee. "Dude," says Dave.

"Dude," I carefully respond, pretty much nailing my intended salutation of "Beautiful day to be alive, isn't it? Play well." But for some reason I am not finished. "Hell," I add, provoking a puzzled look from Dave.

"Dude," Hugh tries, missing badly in my estimation.

"Dude." "Dude!" "*Dude.*" All of us attempt to speak to Dave in his own language before his group hits their balls, leaving just the three of us on the tee box.

The talk is small. And sparse. Sam likes to concentrate on the game when he's in contention, and I continue to be less than a chatterbox. Kevin was a high school valedictorian also voted Most Likely To Succeed. Even more impressive, he can let you know this without having you dislike him. A guy like that would ordinarily find a way to keep an entertaining conversation going—except that there is the matter of what transpired the last time we golfed together. Finally, though, with Sam walking down the opposite side of the fairway, he tells me he has something important to say.

"I hope it's OK to bring it up, but in case this is an issue between us, I want to reassure you that you don't owe me a laptop. I dried it out, and it fired up just fine."

This is pretty funny, and it's delivered so well, and my mental health is so solid, that I have no choice but to laugh.

"All right!" he says. "Stop me when this becomes gamesmanship."

"So," he continues, "how much do you know about the night of infamy?"

"Gamesmanship."

"I'm serious. What has Syd told you?"

"Nothing. I wouldn't let her talk about it. I didn't want to hear a word. Still don't." I never maintained, even to myself, that such a position isn't stupid and juvenile, only that there are some things a person is allowed to be stupid and juvenile about.

"You don't know everything you should, then." Kevin is threatening to crash my arty little film festival with a screening of something gory.

"OK, so I'm at the course having beers with you and the guys when my phone rings. It's Carrie, telling me to come pick her up at your place, where she's been having a couple of drinks with Syd. We're due somewhere for dinner at 7:30, so I have to get straight over. Except, when I show up at the door, Carrie opens it with just a towel on, which, true to form, she unwraps.

They're loaded, and they've been in the hot tub. Not Syd's fault, I'm sure, but it's clear there's been some flirting. Syd's obviously embarrassed, but she's also pretty drunk and maybe a little high, and when Carrie comes up behind her and starts rubbing her shoulders and stroking her hair, she just closes her eyes and lies back in the tub."

My suspicions would be aroused by the neatness of this story and its uncanny resemblance to a hotel-room movie selection I recall once having made, except for the single extraneous detail involving Syd's hair. It's absolutely true: the simple act of stroking it rendered her powerless to resist, a vulnerability I regularly exploited.

"I don't know where this is all going, but I won't say I'm not enjoying the spectacle, and when Carrie grabs me and pulls me to the tub, I guess I don't refuse. So now the three of us are in there, and we're not keeping to our separate corners. Syd's saying, 'Where's Jeff? I have to call Jeff. We have to stop.' But your phone is turned off, and it's hard for anyone to do anything except enjoy themselves when Carrie has her magic fingers going."

I did have my phone off, and Carrie regularly advised those she knew well of her hearty and omnivorous appetite, so I am going to have to maintain a degree of credulity as Kevin continues his far-fetched story.

"I guess I'm the sober one who should be the voice of reason, but instead I say, 'Jeff will be back soon and then he can join us.' This makes the girls very happy. We're all laughing, 'What a cool surprise!' But it also gives us permission to go a little further."

Kevin is 180 yards out and about to hit a 6-iron, while I'm at 170, and holding my 7. Neither of us is thrilled with his shot.

"And we do go further, Syd and I, it's true. And then suddenly Carrie is pissed off, really pissed off. One second she's the conductor and first violinist, the next she's calling us sluts and jumping out of the tub. She told me she was going to leave her car at your place because she was so drunk, but instead she runs out the door and drives away—and five seconds later you pull up."

"Is this true? Any of it?"

"It's all true. We tried to explain, but the next thing we knew the truck was exploding and the police were there."

We stop talking for a minute, since to save par we both need to make tricky chips, tidily accomplished.

"OK, you're saying I was invited to your little orgy all along, so I shouldn't be upset about what went on. If that were all there was to it, maybe I wouldn't be."

"That is all there was to it."

"But then you and Syd hooked up."

"No. Never."

"Oh, come on."

"Carrie left town pretty much the next day, but that was no big deal. Syd and I were both alone, and I tried to be her friend. She was in a bad way and needed one. But she couldn't forgive me for what we did, and she couldn't forgive herself either. And then there was all that shit going on with you. She was heartbroken; that's the only word for it."

Now, that's gamesmanship, I think to myself. It's hard to play golf when you're all choked up about someone as sweet and apparently nearly semi-blameless as Syd. Nevertheless, I nail my wedge from 132 and walk up to make the tap-in.

"OK, some crossed signals," I say, apparently having decided to balance my reputation for overreaction with a classic bit of understatement. "And no argument that Syd suffered too. But that shit going on with me included losing my job, ending my career and enduring a year of pain and depression. The terrible consequence for you was having to pick out a new Porsche."

Clearly I believe that my hurt feelings have not received their due. Perhaps I also harbor concern that the defining event in my life is being explained away as a stock scene in a bedroom farce.

"Oh, that," he says. "Consider it a nice head start on your new life. You'd be gone from the company by now anyway. Half the staff has been fired, suppliers aren't getting paid, and we're maybe two weeks from Chapter 11. I've got every head hunter in the state shopping me around, but suddenly there's no work anywhere. I just took a 40% pay cut, my stock options are worthless, and you know what my lease is now? A Camry."

"Ouch."

"Yeah."

We've finished the front nine and are back at the clubhouse, where the biggest party of the year is underway. Kevin and I are in at 34, while Sam has only been able to manage par on the front nine. Since no-one in the group in front of us is making a charge, it looks like it will come down to Kevin and me, barring some kind of miracle or collapse.

I spot Syd and Georgia standing together over on the patio, and try to catch Syd's eye. The pair are wearing almost identical yellow sundresses, which must have mortified them both when they first arrived, but only highlights how alike they look, while contributing to the impression that they make for the most striking mother-daughter combination ever. For a time it seemed that Syd and I were somehow going to become good platonic friends even as Jenny and I moved in the opposite direction. But then Jenny high-tailed it and the exes had their little lunch date; even a person as perceptive as me could see how pissed off Syd was.

But now that Kevin has filled me in on so much stuff, I desperately want a chance to talk. Syd is being careful not to notice me, however; she and Georgia are busy fussing over Sam, each with an arm around his back as he grabs a quick sandwich and replenishes his water bottle.

And quickly we must be off again. Sam is really doing his strong, silent thing now, and even Kevin seems to have decided it is time to focus on the game. The second-year member has a one-stroke lead in the club championship, so it's only appropriate that he put a lid on the effervescence. I look for indications of stress when I catch him with a birdie on 12, but either he's not feeling any or I have not magically become a person with insight into the ways of other humans. If I am able to read signs at all, it seems to me it's Sam who is fighting the fatigue and pressure. He's a 66-year-old who's been carrying his bag for 30-odd holes on a blazing summer day, even as his chances of winning get less and less realistic by the minute.

For the final round the pins have been set up as tough as they can be, so all three of us are doing well to scrape out pars. At the 16th we wind back toward the clubhouse, where a rapidly growing and party-hearty crowd has gathered to watch us in. Based on past experience the gallery will follow for 17 and 18 with drinks in hand. Reasonably discreet chatter ensues as word spreads that Kevin and I are tied, with Sam three strokes behind.

I keep trying to catch Syd's eye, but except when she joins Georgia to watch Sam tee off on 17, she manages to lose herself in the crowd. It's strange perhaps, but if there are 400 people on the course, 399 are watching the golfers while one is intently scanning the gallery, which is restricted here to the right side of the tee box. Perhaps because of this I am almost certainly the only person—well, one of two—to notice an upward flash of yellow fabric that's directly in Sam's gaze as he bends down to pick up his tee. I am briefly shocked—until I glimpse the dark triangle that only the older of the two London beauties could possess. Sam's eyeful lasts the same few micro-seconds as mine, but it seems to result in a new sense of purpose. He promptly reaches into his bag and unsheathes that big purple umbrella of his, no doubt to protect himself from the late afternoon glare.

Whatever Sam is feeling, the feeling is working. The 460-yard 17th is set up so tough that Kevin and I are less than devastated when our par putts fail to drop, but Sam astonishingly hits a 4-iron to 12 feet, then sinks the putt for birdie. Then, on the par-5 18th, he nails his biggest drive of the day. It rolls out a good 270 yards, leaving maybe 260 to a hard right pin diabolically positioned mere feet from the club's only artificial water body, a pond that's so pretty and well-incorporated into the landscape that even we minimalists have to cut it some slack. I hit a conservative 3-wood but end up only a couple of yards behind Sam's ball, then Kevin bashes his driver into the thick rough that had been shouting to me, "Don't hit driver! Don't hit driver!" This is the opening I have been waiting for. Kevin will have to gouge out, leaving himself a long iron to that nasty and dangerous pin. Meanwhile, with my 3-wood I can outhit Sam by a good 20 yards, and he's a stroke behind me anyway. The way the pond is angled, only I can reach the nice patch of flat ground just off the left front edge of the green. If I make this one straightforward shot I will give myself a solid birdie chance and almost certain victory.

Sure enough, I hit a soaring shot that catches enough of the downslope to bounce almost onto the left edge of the green, maybe 75 feet from the pin. Unable to get anywhere a person would want to be with his own 3-wood, Sam will now have to lay up short of the water with an iron—except what's this? It would be wrong for me to gasp, but fortunately the gallery is doing it for me. That isn't an iron in Sam's hand, or even a potentially foolish fairway wood, but a driver. Yes, the six-time club champion, the oldest man left standing by almost three full decades, is going to attempt one of the rarest shots in the game, an act of bravado or desperation that never fails to excite the announcers who cover the Tour. He's going to hit driver off the deck.

Sam has handed the umbrella to Georgia, and she gives it a little twirl as he takes a stance calculated to produce a big fade. Syd, who has been carrying his bag these last two holes while still managing to ignore me, stands next to her mom. I hear the crack and watch as Syd and Georgia stare intently at the ball's flat arc, then grab each other in a touching display of familial intimacy. If ever mother and daughter failed to get along, there is no inkling of it now. Sam has hit a crazy slice that finds the very top of the hill far off to the left and then bounces hard right towards the green, dexterously skirting the water. The gallery is literally roaring, and I don't have to squint my eyes to know where the ball has come to rest. There are only a few people down at the green, but we can hear them hooting and laughing. One of them holds up his arms, giving us the measurement: less than a foot. Sam has left himself a kick-in eagle.

Kevin proceeds to dunk his 5-iron, which means the hole is playing out precisely as I imagined, except for the small matter of Sam's eagle. Still, I have an eagle putt of my own, which would win it, and I need only get up and down to send the match into extra holes. There's more cheering, then clapping, and then that settles into a rhythmic beat, finally giving away to a chant of, "Sam, Sam, Sam," as we walk up to the green. Not that I had any illusions, but it appears I am not the crowd favorite. Kevin takes his drop, pitches to 20 feet, then putts out to leave the stage to us, as I assess my putt from the fringe.

This will be a big sweeper, breaking maybe 30 feet from left to right. The first half will be slow, but the second part will run blindingly fast as it catches the slope down to the water. Well, no worries. I should make a two-putt like this maybe 80 percent of the time, and all that negative energy willing me to roll it off the green and into the water fails to bother me as I take care to loosen my grip on the putter handle and make the necessary stroke. The ball needs to almost stop on the crest of the hill 20 feet above the cup, and that is what it does before just catching the slope and picking up speed once again. It's a good putt, but I have hit it a touch too strong, as was almost certain to be the case. It misses a half-foot left before coming to rest maybe six feet past.

I catch a glimpse of Syd, who continues to be glued to Georgia, making for an impressive study in yellowness. There will be no magic show for me today, nor do I need any. All I need is to correctly read this mere six-footer, then make the stroke. In my favor I have played this green thousands of times. Working against me, it is the first time I have ever seen this fabled pin position, which is used only once a year, during the final round of the club championship. Is the putt dead straight? The path of my last one on its way by the hole would seem to suggest so, even as logic contends it might turn a little left, and a visual appraisal argues for a half-cup right. When no break can be read, the correct course is usually to aim center cup, and that is what I resolve to do. I make my stroke and watch as the ball heads straight home. Except that with inches to go it edges slightly rightward, bumps a little over the poa annua, curls along the lip, makes as if to drop side door, then comes to rest hanging over the uphill side of the cup.

There is a collective gasp, but the drunken throng succeeds in remembering its etiquette, remaining mostly quiet while I wait out the 10 seconds I am allowed in the hope the ball might drop. When it doesn't, and I swipe the thing in, there follows a round of applause that I have to assess as being precisely appropriate for a second-place finisher who has mounted a stiff challenge.

Ten seconds later the place erupts as Sam makes his tap-in. Kevin and I manage to get in our handshakes with Sam before the green fills with well-wishers led by Georgia and Syd, who get huge hugs from a man who at this moment easily reigns as the world's happiest. And honestly, more power to him, my first and best student, and one of my favorite all-time humans.

Kevin and I find ourselves standing together beside our bags as the celebration begins to take on characteristics more familiar from watching walk-off homers end the seventh game of the World Series. "Never imagined that," Kevin says.

"Sure didn't," I say. "Well, maybe I did."

"You must have seen something I missed."

"You could say that."

But suddenly I am very, very tired. Waking up at 4. Walking 36 holes in the hot sun. The pressure of the match. The conversation with Kevin. The frustration and indeed sadness of not being able to get even a hello out of Syd. And of course, losing such an important tournament when winning seemed so certain.

"See you in church," I say to Kevin, after checking and signing the official scorecard that he has been marking for the three of us. "I have to get some rest."

I stop for something to eat and to pick up some things, so it is after 10 and very dark out by the time I get back to the apartment. Tomorrow I will have to be up early to manage the business, which is now Bill-less. There will be students to instruct, cajole and negotiate with, and a lawsuit that needs attending to. Looking beyond the next 24 hours, life appears to be good, or at least acceptable. Even from Denmark my mother will no doubt do something to bug me, but I expect we will have pleasant moments, too. Jenny is gone forever, but the magic of Craigslist persists.

When I turn on the laptop there are messages waiting. Three are responses to my new ad, in which I have portrayed myself as the gentlemanly owner of a sports-related business who is interested mostly in visiting wine-tasting rooms and long walks at sunset. Jenny vetted it from afar and assured me that casual encounters would quickly ensue.

Another is from Bill, and it's short but sweet. "Hi Jeff. Congratulations on winning the club championship! (I assume!!) Your mom and I just visited that other Tivoli place, and it's even nicer than ours! Hope all's well at the new range. Let me know if there's anything I can do. P.S. You wouldn't believe it, there are Hans Wegner chairs everywhere!!"

That's a lot of exclamation marks, even for a car dealer.

The final message, just a few minutes old, is from Syd, and it's even sweeter.

"Jeff, I'm glad you had a chance to talk with Kevin. I'm so sorry I missed you. I would have liked to tell you how well you played and what a great teacher you've become.

"Hey, up for nine at the club some evening? Please say yes. I've got something to show you."

Yes. Hell, yes.

ABOUT THE AUTHOR

Jim Sutherland spent two decades as an editor at magazines in the U.S. and Canada, including *Institutional Investor*, *Western Living* and *Vancouver magazine*, which was named Canada's Magazine of the Year in 1997, while he was editor in chief. In May 2007, about the time this story begins, he left *Institutional Investor* to write for magazines and websites on design and architecture, food and wine, travel, business and, at every chance, golf. He lives in Vancouver, B.C., and this is his first novel.

www.jimsutherland.net